Ali Sparkes

UNLEASHED

MIND OVER MATTER

OXFORD

UNIVERSITY PRESS

OXFORD

UNIVERSITY PRESS

Great Clarendon Street, Oxford OX2 6DP

Oxford University Press is a department of the University of Oxford.
It furthers the University's objective of excellence in research, scholarship,
and education by publishing worldwide in

Oxford New York

Auckland Cape Town Dar es Salaam Hong Kong Karachi
Kuala Lumpur Madrid Melbourne Mexico City Nairobi
New Delhi Shanghai Taipei Toronto

With offices in

Argentina Austria Brazil Chile Czech Republic France Greece
Guatemala Hungary Italy Japan Poland Portugal Singapore
South Korea Switzerland Thailand Turkey Ukraine Vietnam

Oxford is a registered trade mark of Oxford University Press
in the UK and in certain other countries

British Library Cataloguing in Publication Data

Data available

ISBN: 978-0-19-275607-7

1 3 5 7 9 10 8 6 4 2

Printed in Great Britain

Paper used in the production of this book is a natural,
recyclable product made from wood grown in sustainable forests.
The manufacturing process conforms to the environmental
regulations of the country of origin.

**For Rosie—another brave, resourceful
redhead!**

With grateful thanks to Neil White for his
guidance on special operations and tech and to
Charlie for additional special ops insight.

1

A tiny avalanche of pebbles tumbled down the cliff face. They rattled musically as they bounced off large chunks of chalk, flint, and clay.

'Go on,' said Gideon, staring up at the ribbed grey curve of the Best Ammonite In The World. 'Keep going. Left and right . . . ge-e-ently . . . '

Luke nodded and held his sightline as if his pale green eyes were lasers boring into the cliff. And, in a manner of speaking, they were. The ammonite, five or six metres up in the crumbly strata, nudged a little to the left.

'Keeeeep it coming,' said Gideon, rubbing his hands through his fluffy blond hair in tense concentration. 'As soon as it's out I'll catch it and bring it down safely . . . Yeeees . . . Just a bit further down. A biiiit furthe—*DOOF*!'

CRACK! The impact between his shoulder blades was so sudden and so forceful that the air was knocked out of his lungs and he was smacked face down into the gritty foot of the cliff. He was dimly aware that Luke had executed the same manoeuvre and as he scrambled round to see their attacker his brother did likewise, a mirror image to his right.

Both of them were hauled up into a standing position and roughly shaken by one shoulder. Only one man held them but they knew better than to attempt to struggle out of the iron grip.

'Wh-what?' squawked Gideon, trying to sound indignant rather than guilty.

It didn't work.

'Try me!' rumbled the heavy-browed man who had them immobilized. 'Just once more.'

'U-Uncle Jem!' Gideon's eyes skittered around, trying to remind the man that the beach had people on it. *Normal* people. Admittedly, probably only about two dozen sprinkled out along the mile or so of pebbly shore, but still . . . *people.* 'We were just looking at the fossils!'

'You were not just looking,' growled the man, his Scottish accent deepening. Gideon had noticed that it got much more distinct when Jem

2

was angry or stressed. 'Don't take me for an idiot, Gideon. One more trick like that and you'll be on a helicopter back to Cumbria before you can say *Oh—what happened to my holiday?*'

Gideon gulped. He stared down at his feet in their surfer-dude-style beach sandals and sighed. 'Sorry,' he muttered. Luke said nothing—but he *looked* sorry. At last Jem relaxed his grip on their shoulders.

'What's going on in your heads?' he demanded. He took off his baseball cap, revealing close-cropped dark hair, and adjusted the almost invisible communication device inside it. 'How long have you waited for this week? Luke—you know how much it means to your mum. And yet you try to pull a Cola stunt—for what? A chunk of rock?'

Luke looked very guilty. It *had* been incredibly hard to get a week away from Fenton Lodge, their very exclusive, very private college in Cumbria. The preparations had been intense and incredibly complicated, he and Gideon knew that. It had been months—years even—since he had spent time at home on the Isle of Wight with his mum. She had been so excited and delighted. And so of course they had promised not to . . .

'Well . . . it's not just a rock. It's an ammonite actually,' Gideon couldn't help correcting. 'A really big one. Worth a mint! And . . . I . . . should really . . . just shut up now . . . ' Gideon shoved his hands into his shorts pocket and clamped his blabbery mouth into a tight, safe line. He and Luke had just tried to prise an ammonite out of a high cliff face and safely float the fossil down through the air using telekinetic power. In public. He could see that Jem had a point.

'This whole week is only happening on condition that *nobody* gets the slightest idea that you two are not completely normal, ordinary teenage boys,' Jem went on, putting the cap back on with an angry tug. 'Normal ordinary teenage boys do not move things around with their minds.' He exhaled sharply and shook his head. 'I *told* Control this was a mistake. I think we should end this now.'

He went to press a tiny connector in the cap just above his right ear and opened his mouth to report in to Control. Luke raised his hands in horror and Gideon pleaded, 'No! Jem! Please don't! We're sorry. I promise you we will not do it again. I promise!'

Jem paused and narrowed his dark grey eyes at

them. He regarded them for some time and then let his hand drop. 'It's bad enough that I have to babysit you two for a week and pretend to be your uncle,' he muttered. 'I didn't expect to have to discipline you as well.'

'You won't have to—not again!' said Gideon. 'We'll be good—perfect!'

Jem let a hint of a smile touch his mouth. 'Well—*that* wouldn't be normal and teenage would it?'

Luke grinned, sighing with relief. They'd only been here since yesterday and it would have broken Mum's heart if they'd been whisked back up country less than twenty-four hours later.

'Come on, the others are getting twitchy. Let's go and get some ice cream.' Jem turned round and headed across the beach towards a young couple who were stretched out on some beach mats. He didn't stop at their beach camp though, but just walked on along to the foot of the zigzagging cliff path, where some enterprising Islanders had set up an ice cream kiosk and a burger and hot dog stand.

Gideon glanced at the young couple. The man, fair haired and tanned, was lying flat on his back, sunglasses shading his eyes, soaking up the early summer heat on his bare chest. He appeared to be asleep, but Gideon and Luke knew better. The woman, slim, dark haired, and pretty, in shorts and a halter-neck bikini top, a wide brimmed hat on her head, was sitting up, apparently reading a paperback. Gideon wanted to say hi, but again, knew better. As they moved on he heard a sigh and saw the woman put a bookmark into the paperback. She knew her morning's beach lounging could be over at any time, especially with Gideon, Luke, and their 'Uncle' Jem on the move.

Jem had bought them some cones already, topped with a mound of fluffy white Island ice cream, each planted with a chocolate flake. They moved to a bench halfway up the cliff path to eat them, gazing back down to the beach with its sprinkling of people, brightly coloured towels, and wind breaks. Two old ladies were in fold-out chairs not far from the ice cream kiosk. The young couple they'd passed were packing up their beach mats and getting ready to go. Several bold swimmers were up to their waists in the chilly June surf. A girl with a dog was exploring one of the outcrops of pale chalky cliff face, digging at it with something and putting her finds in a battered satchel bag hanging over her shoulder. The dog—a wiry little black thing—ran up and down the slope of the crumbled cliff footings.

'They do find some amazing stuff here,' said Jem after a few minutes of companionable ice cream slurping. 'Last year, after a storm, they uncovered an almost complete brachiosaur skeleton.'

Gideon let out a sigh as he remembered the Best Ammonite In The World. If only he and Luke could have got it down. It was as big as a bike wheel and would have fetched hundreds, he felt sure of it, at one of the fossil shops. He glanced back along the cliff face to where he and Luke had tried *just a little bit* of Cola power. Last night's rain had loosened it off nicely. If they'd had just *one* more minute.

'Forget it, Gideon,' said Jem, as if reading his mind. 'It would have taken at least half an hour to get it out. There would have been a pretty good sized crowd around you by then. Local paper. Isle of Wight TV. International terrorists on their way. You know the drill.'

'Yes—I know!' muttered Gideon. He didn't like being reminded how difficult normal life was for Colas. There were just over a hundred Children Of Limitless Ability. All aged between 13 and 15. All suddenly blessed (or cursed) with some

7

extraordinary talent when they were 11 or 12. Some, like he and Luke, were telekinetics. Others, like their friend Lisa, could read minds and talk to the spirit world. Some could create illusions, vanish, communicate by telepathy—or heal broken bones, like their friend Mia. One—and one only—could shapeshift. Gideon's best friend, Dax. He was prouder than he could ever express to have the world's only shapeshifter for a best friend. He was also proud of his brother. Luke. The strong and silent one.

It might sound amazing—and it was. But their astonishing powers were also a big problem. Protected and educated by a *very* special government department, the Colas were Britain's most precious assets. They could be incredibly powerful. And also incredibly dangerous. And unfortunately it was more than rumour, beyond the walls of Fenton Lodge estate, that they existed.

Which is why, after months of wrangling, this innocent week-long holiday on the Isle of Wight could only happen with a minimum of *three* SAS-trained government minders in tow. Jem was one of them, posing as their uncle. The couple on the beach were the other two.

On top of that, Gideon and Luke had to have tracker chips in their clothes and shoes. They were transported here by helicopter, directly from the grounds of Fenton Lodge. And even then, only after one of them had made a supreme sacrifice.

One of them had to dye.

Gideon grinned at Luke as he worked his way down the last little finger of cone. 'Suits you,' he chuckled, flicking his brother's black hair. Luke rolled his eyes. When Mrs Dann, one of their teachers at Fenton Lodge, had first presented Gideon with a box of L'Oréal Excellence, with a picture of a raven-haired beauty on it, Gideon had freaked.

'Sorry,' said Mrs Dann, trying not *very* hard not to laugh. 'But identical, blond twins out and about are just too noticeable on a small island. You've got to untwin.'

'But he's got glasses on!' protested Gideon, pointing, unnecessarily, to the specs on Luke's nose. 'That's enough, isn't it?'

Dax had fallen backwards over the sofa, he was laughing so hard. Lisa stepped up to peer at the box, stroking her own long blonde hair and beaming. 'Ooh! It conditions as well as colours,

Gideon. Oh go on . . . *because you're worth it*!'

In the end Luke had taken the box out of his hands and gone upstairs with Mrs Dann to change his hair colour. On his return to the common room an hour later there had been whoops of delight and derision. But not for long. Weirdly, Luke looked quite good with black hair.

'Oooh—Gothic!' Jennifer had said, before vanishing by the fire. A few seconds later Luke had felt her fingers tugging at the fluffy blackness. She squealed with mirth when he flapped his arms around to find her, and reappeared by the fire five seconds later, trying to look innocent.

Girls! thought Gideon as he munched his last bit of cone. His eyes wandered back along the foot of the cliff where that girl with the little dog was now crouching down, digging vigorously at something in the crumbly Wealden clay. She had shoulder length auburn hair which floated in the breeze. Every so often she would impatiently tuck a strand of it back behind her ear. Her shorts and T-shirt were grubby with chalk and clay and she had some kind of ankle boots on—battered brown things with rugged soles. She did not look like a day tripper. Her limbs were lean and golden brown from regular days outdoors and she seemed entirely at ease with her task. Completely focused even when she was absent-mindedly ruffling her dog's head with one hand.

Gideon decided he fancied her. He nudged Luke and pointed down, waggling his eyebrows for effect. Luke looked and then smiled and moved his hands descriptively.

'Yup,' said Gideon. 'Definitely a bit of a babe. A rock chick. Geddit?'

Luke laughed silently.

And that was when Gideon first noticed the crack at the top of the cliff.

Three seconds later the cliff began to fall.

2

Lydia Carr was having a bad morning. She'd been digging in the cliffs for more than two hours now but all she'd found were titchy ammonites, broken sharks' teeth, and more fossilized crocodile poo than she could realistically hope to sell. She was getting hungry and the small sandwich in her satchel was calling already . . . but she really wanted to wait until midday at least before eating it. She had to make food last. She took the satchel off and set it to one side so she wouldn't be tempted.

Fish was in a funny mood today too. He kept coming up and nudging her with his little black head, trying to get her to go. 'Gettoff, Fish!' she muttered as he tried again and she was surprised to feel his teeth on her arm. Not biting—Fish would never bite her—but grasping hold of her as if he'd found something exciting to show her and was wanting her to come with him. But Fish wasn't any good at spotting fossils or minerals. 'I can't come now,' she said, working her chisel hard into the chalky rock. 'This looks like a geode!'

Fish barked. Something else he rarely did. And for the first time Lydia turned to look at him, concerned. He was shaking and urging her to get up and go—she could tell this by the way he was moving.

'WHAT?' she demanded, standing up and resting her filthy hands on her hips, the chisel at her feet. 'What is the problem—GAH!'

She never got to finish her query. At that moment she was shoved sideways as if she'd been hit by a small truck. She screamed, tumbling through the air, dimly aware that the small truck was actually another human being. Somebody had attacked her! Here—in broad daylight!

And the attack wasn't over. The fair haired boy grabbed her arms and dragged her up again before throwing her bodily down the scree of rocks and stones and sand. She screamed again and rolled away from the next strike. The boy was running for her, his face wild, yelling something at her. Why didn't somebody come to help her? There were people on this beach!

The boy threw himself at her again, knocking her mouth with his shoulder and crushing her into the sand with his entire body weight. She kicked and struggled and tried to bite his arm. Where was Fish? Why wasn't he defending her?

It was only now, as she strained to hear Fish barking, that she noticed the noise. The *other* noise, above the shuddering breathing and shouting from the boy pinning her to the beach and her own yowls of fury. It was a deep, rumbling, rasping sound. And now she could feel shaking too.

'Let it GO!' yelled the boy, not to her, but to someone else, further along the beach. 'It's OK!'

And then the rumbling, rasping sound intensified and the ground beneath her was trembling. Oh no! A *collapse*! A landslip! The sound seemed to echo off the cliffs and sea and then, after probably just ten seconds, it died away and an unearthly silence filled the air, punctuated only by the jingle and ping of tiny pebbles coming to rest.

She was scrunching her eyes up tight, scared to look. She could feel debris on her legs, but it didn't seem heavy. The boy got up and stood over her, blocking out the dust-filtered sun. 'Are you OK?' he asked in a voice that sounded as shocked as she felt.

She sat up and spat sand out. 'What . . . the hell . . . ?'

'I'm sorry—I didn't mean to hurt you. There was no time to explain.' He waved a hand at the devastation behind him. A huge chunk of the cliff had collapsed. Tonnes and tonnes of rock and chalk and clay and vegetation lay in a surreal stew, pulverized particles rising from it like steam, exactly where she and Fish had been only forty-five seconds ago.

'FISH!' she screamed, scrambling to her feet. 'FISH!'

The boy peered at her, one fair eyebrow up, confused. 'The fish will be OK,' he said slowly. 'The cliff didn't hit the water.'

'No, you idiot!' she squawked. 'FISH! My *dog*! Where is he? Where is he?' A sob caught in her throat. Poor Fish. He'd been trying to warn her. He must have known, in the way that animals sometimes do, that the landslip was coming. He'd tried to tell her . . . and she had ignored him and now . . .

15

She heard a yelping noise and spun round to see another boy coming towards her, carrying . . .

'*FISH!*' she cried, running. 'Oh, thank you!' She reached the other boy, who had black hair and glasses, and seized the small shaggy form from him. A tall, muscular man in a baseball cap was close behind him, watching intently. 'Are you OK?' She squeezed Fish tight and he licked her nose.

'Are *you* OK?' repeated the blond boy and she turned to look at him properly. He had a nice face—lightly freckled, with pale green eyes and a mouth that looked ready to laugh—although right now it was tight with concern.

'I—I'm fine,' she said. 'Thank you. I think you just saved my life. And Fish's.'

The boy snorted. 'What kind of name is *that* for a dog?' he laughed.

She smiled back. 'It's the name my little brother gave him. He *was* four. Don't ask me why! It kind of stuck . . . Is . . . is anybody else caught in that?' Her eyes were drawn back to the landslip. The beach around them was rapidly emptying as the small number of visitors scrambled up the stable end of the cliff, along the zigzag path, many on mobile phones, dialing 999 or filming the landslip. A few more, though, were hurrying back down the path towards the landslip, agog to see it.

'No,' said the boy. 'Only you and . . . er . . . Fish were on that part of the beach.'

'And you,' she said. 'I guess you happened to be looking up at the right moment.'

'You could say that,' he beamed. 'We both,' he nodded across to the dark-haired boy, 'noticed and did what we could to help. I'm Gideon by the way. And . . . I know *this* is Fish . . . '

He leaned across and comically shook Fish's small scratchy paw, before holding his hand out to her.

'I'm Lydia,' she said, feeling the shudders of alarm gradually start to abate as their bizarre, polite conversation continued. Only minutes ago this boy had mashed her into the sand with a full body drop—and now she was shaking his hand as if they were guests at a dinner party.

'And this is Luke,' said Gideon as the other boy stepped forward and offered his hand too, with a smile. 'And our uncle—Jem.' The man nodded and smiled at her, tucking his hands into his shorts pockets. He seemed tense, thought Lydia. But then, his nephews *had* nearly been crushed by a falling cliff, so that wasn't surprising.

'Thanks for getting Fish for me,' she said, smiling at Luke. He had the same pale green eyes behind his glasses, so most likely was Gideon's brother. He smiled back at her but didn't say anything.

'Um . . . Luke can't speak,' explained Gideon.

'Oh,' she nodded. 'I'm sorry. THANK YOU—FOR SAVING—FISH!' She spoke slowly and loudly, enunciating each word with care. To her surprise Gideon let off another snort of laughter and Luke bit his lip, looking highly amused.

'I didn't say he was *deaf*,' said Gideon, clapping his brother on the shoulder. 'He just can't *speak*.'

'Oh.' She felt extremely foolish. 'Sorry . . .'

'Don't worry,' said Gideon. 'It happens all the time. Especially as we do sign a bit.' He moved his hands expressively in the air, marking out strange shapes and quick, understated mimes. Luke did the same back, varying the shapes and glancing across at her more than once.

'He says you're welcome,' grinned Gideon. 'And that Fish is the best name for a dog he's ever heard.'

'Well . . . it was nice meeting you,' she said, unsure of exactly what to do next. 'I'd better . . . get along. Have to get to the fossil shop.'

'The fossil shop?' said Gideon. 'Do you work there?' He scanned her features and she knew he was wondering if she was old enough to work in a shop. She was . . . but only just, being 14.

'No . . . I sell them the fossils I find,' she explained. 'I'd better get these to them.' And she glanced down at her satchel, only to be hit with another punch of shock. No satchel. 'Oh NO! My satchel . . . and my tools! NO!' She gazed across at the settling landslip and wailed, tugging her hands through her gritty hair. And then she dropped Fish and ran.

'STOP! Are you NUTS?' yelled Gideon. 'You can't go over there! It's dangerous.'

But she *was* going over there. She had to. She had to get her satchel and her tools. She could live without the fossils—paltry as they had been today—but she could never afford to replace the tools. She leapt across the churned-up ground, jumping from clump to clump of wrecked strata, keeping her eyes open for potholes and small crumbling chasms that might lead to a further collapse or a twisted ankle. Mid-way through one of these leaps she was seized by both arms and brought to a sudden halt. It was the man—their uncle. He pulled her to a complete stop and stood, immovable, for a few seconds while she struggled and then gave up trying to move on, another sob escaping her throat.

'Don't be an idiot,' he said, with a Scottish accent. 'You know the geology of this place, don't you? You know how dangerous it is here right now.'

'Let me go . . . ' She felt her rib cage tremble as she tried to get the words out. 'You don't understand. That . . . that bag. Those tools. They're all I have. All I have to make our money.'

The uncle turned her to face him and narrowed dark grey eyes at her beneath his cap. He seemed to read something in her face, because he gave a small, sharp nod and said, 'Wait here. Sit.' He pushed her down onto a cracked boulder of Wealden clay and then moved cautiously across the crumpled rockscape beneath the brand new cliff face. He leant over and tugged at something which snaked up out of the debris. Brown. A strap. He'd found her bag! Just like that!

'Must have been thrown up in the impact,' he said, making his way back to her. 'I found this too. Yours?' And wonder of wonders, he handed her the chisel, too.

'Thank you *so* much,' she said, wiping her eyes

and leaving a smear of tears across the mud and dust on her cheek.

'You should go home,' said the uncle, steering her round and back towards Gideon and Luke who were waiting anxiously at the edge of the landslip with Fish. 'Have some sweet tea and a rest. You're a bit in shock.'

She nodded. 'Yes. I will go.'

'Come up the path with us now,' he said, as they rejoined the boys and Fish jumped up at her, anxiously resting his paws on her knees.

'No . . . Thanks—but I live that way.' She pointed to the far end of the beach where a distant path meandered up a shallower incline of grassy dunes, about a mile away. 'I'm fine now. Thank you— all of you.' She nodded, slipping the chisel into her bag and then, throwing the satchel over her shoulder, heedless of the bleeding scrapes and bruises and thick coating of dust and grit all over her, marched away from them towards the firm shingle near the water's edge. Fish trotted after her, tail wagging.

Jem looked at Luke and Gideon and shook his head. The thud of a helicopter rearing up across the sea made the brothers gulp and stare at him.

'Is that for us?' said Gideon, looking grey. 'Did you call Control?'

Jem turned away from the water and began to walk towards the cliff path. 'No, I didn't call Control. That's a coastguard helicopter checking out the cliff fall. Come on—it'll be swarming with emergency services here any minute.'

'So . . . you're not going to report us,' said Gideon. 'Even though we did Cola stuff. *Massive* Cola stuff.'

Jem turned back to face them and there was something unreadable about his expression. 'You . . . you just changed the laws of physics,' he stated, staring at Luke. 'You stood there and you *looked* at it . . . and you held back a *falling cliff*.'

Luke nodded, biting his lip. He and Gideon had both held back the cliff, in fact, gripping each other's arms and locking their eyes onto the awful crack which had suddenly opened up just twenty metres away from their perch. As soon as they had steadied it, Gideon had carefully pulled back his telekinetic power, allowing Luke to take over. They could each sense the strength needed and once they'd realized that one of them could hold it for maybe forty-five seconds, Gideon had run down the path to get that girl out of the way.

'We're sorry,' said Gideon. 'But we couldn't just let—'

'—a girl and her dog get crushed to death,' finished Jem. 'I know. Nor could I.' He glanced up the path. At the top the young couple, who were actually Jem's back-up special operatives, were watching carefully.

'I just hope,' said Jem, 'that nobody saw.'

Half a mile down the beach Lydia sank onto the sand and took some deep, hitching breaths as the delayed shock hit her. Then, with a shaking hand, she opened up the satchel and found, amid the precious tools and the poor fossil crop, a squashed thin parcel of tin foil. Inside it her single cheese sandwich was like paste. She scraped it out and forced herself to eat it, washing it down with lukewarm water from an old plastic lemonade bottle. She gave one bite to Fish and poured the dregs of the water over his flappy pink tongue.

Peering back along the beach, she thought she could see the man and two boys disappearing over the headland. Good. That uncle of theirs . . . he worried her. He seemed like . . . authority. She got up and walked back the way she'd come, retracing her steps and heading for home in the same direction as her rescuers after all, planning, as she passed it, the route back to the landslip at dawn tomorrow. Dangerous or not, the best fossil finds were always unearthed in newborn landslips. She could not afford to miss that chance.

3

'No, nothing to do with us,' said Jem. Control was clearly not convinced. 'Look, landslips happen all the time around here,' he added. 'It's one of the most eroded coastlines in the British Isles. That's why they keep finding dinosaurs. The cliff just fell.'

'And neither Gideon nor Luke were using their talents?' said Control. 'You're quite sure?'

'Nothing made that cliff fall except three days of rain,' insisted Jem.

'But the fact remains, something extraordinary occurred there and the Reader twins *just happened* to be on the beach.'

Jem gritted his teeth and clenched his fingers around the phone. 'I've told you what happened. It's my judgement that there is nothing to worry about. If you disagree, send the transport and we'll all head back.' He paused and whoever it was who was running Control today did not respond. 'But understand this, Chambers will get a full report and whichever red-tape chewing over-reacting drone stopped this holiday will have to answer for it. Colas are this country's greatest asset. If we don't look after them we'll lose them—and I don't know about *you*, Control, but one lousy week on the Isle of Wight in three years is hardly the high life, now is it?'

A few more seconds of silence passed on the end of the line and then Control concluded, 'Keep us posted,' and abruptly hung up.

'Come and eat, Jem,' said Annie, touching him gently on the shoulder. 'Cottage pie and peas!' She smiled at him and he smiled back, appreciatively. Luke's adoptive mother was a very good cook. He joined the small family at the table in the cottage kitchen and helped himself to two big dollops of cottage pie and a good sprinkling of peas.

'Gideon's been telling me all about your cliff drama,' said Annie. She was a heavy-set woman in her late fifties, with grey-flecked dark hair kept tucked back in a bun, pale blue eyes, and a warm smile. 'I'm always saying there should be more checks along the south and east coastlines. Someone could so easily have been walking along the top when it went. Terrifying!' She took one hand of each boy and squeezed, proudly. 'Thank goodness you were both there.'

'Yes,' said Jem. 'And that will be *all* the Cola activity finished now for this holiday. Right, boys?'

Gideon and Luke nodded back at him, solemnly.

'Remember—we cannot attract attention,' he added, for what seemed like the fiftieth time.

'We won't, we promise!' said Gideon. 'The island hardly knows we're here.'

'Apart from that young lady you saved,' said Annie. 'I doubt *she'll* forget you in a hurry.'

'Well, she lives miles away,' said Gideon. 'We'll never see her again. So—tomorrow! Castle or zoo? Or both?'

'I can manage the zoo,' said Annie. 'But the castle's a bit too much climbing for me. Why don't you do Carisbrooke in the morning with Jem and then come back for me and we can do the zoo and have tea afterwards?'

'Sounds like a plan,' said Jem, running his eye over the County Press newspaper as he forked some cottage pie into his mouth. Gideon could tell he was bored. This was not exactly the level of operation he was used to—hanging around with two kids pretending to be an uncle. Not the most challenging assignment he'd had this year. Nevertheless, Jem knew it was a privilege to be asked to handle Cola security detail. Only the very best were ever called for it. A Cola minder had to be prepared for the unexpected.

Gideon regarded Jem with interest, glugging some cloudy lemonade. He wished sometimes that he had a bit of Lisa's talent. Not the talking to dead people bit—yeesh, he could certainly live without *that*—but being able to nip into someone's mind and rummage through their uppermost thoughts and innermost memories. Now *that* would be a very handy skill. He'd love to know what really went on in Jem's mind—and he bet his memories would be explosive stuff after all those years in the Special Air Services.

Luke seemed to be thinking the same. It was odd how often their expressions mirrored, even when they were not looking at each other. As Gideon glanced back at his dark-haired twin he saw the same thoughts crossing Luke's face like waves across a beach. Luke looked up at him and then signed, *Do you think he knew Owen?*

'Did you ever work with Owen Hind, Jem?' asked Gideon.

Jem glanced up from the *County Press.* 'Yes. I was out in the Gulf with him years ago. He was an excellent soldier. The very best.' He dropped his eyes. 'I was at his funeral, although I don't imagine you remember me. You were all pretty cut up that day.'

'We were,' agreed Gideon.

'Was Owen Hind that teacher of yours?' asked Annie. 'The one who died falling off the North Sea oil rig?'

'Yeah,' said Gideon and he and Luke both began to eat again, concentrating hard on the food. Not because they were still experiencing grief over the loss of Owen—their teacher, mentor, friend— because they weren't. For the simple reason that Owen wasn't dead.

Only a handful of people knew this. To the British government, who had laid on the funeral with full military honours, Owen was long gone, killed in the line of duty while protecting the Colas during an attempted abduction. But Dax Jones had learned the truth—that Owen had been saved but chose to remain 'dead' to everyone but Dax and his closest friends. He was alive and well in Spain along with his friend and Gideon's former telekinesis tutor Tyrone Lewis, but it was a secret which Gideon and Luke could *never* reveal.

'That must have been so hard for you all,' Annie went on. 'I know you all really loved Owen.'

'Dax most of all,' said Gideon. 'But he's OK now.'

'Dax is the shapeshifter, yes?' asked Annie.

'Yeah—he turns into a fox or a falcon or an otter,' said Gideon.

'That's just *so* amazing.' Annie shook her head.

Luke prodded his mother's arm and signed indignantly.

'What? Go slower!' she said, trying to read his fluid hands. She had been working hard on signing too. Not because Luke needed her to sign to him but because she needed to understand *his* signing. She could follow quite a bit now.

'He says "are you saying *we're* not as amazing as a shapeshifter?",' grinned Gideon.

Annie chortled and cuffed Luke's wild black hair. 'You're the most amazing thing on this planet,' she reassured him. 'You both are.'

'That's the truth!' muttered Jem, glancing darkly

at his charges and trying to keep any fondness out of his expression. He didn't quite manage it and Gideon realized this was probably why he'd been reminded of Owen. Here was another soldier trying to keep it all professional and not get too involved. Well . . . it was just for a few days. Jem wasn't likely to suffer too much for liking his 'assets' in that time.

After their late lunch Luke and Gideon ambled out into the back garden. Annie's cottage was in the small seaside town of Bonchurch, halfway up a steep hill. Between the trees at the far end of the sloping lawn, the blue of the sea could be glimpsed, gleaming invitingly in the late afternoon sun. Gideon elbowed his way past blossomy shrubs, skirting the small pond set into its ledge of island rock, and ran on down to the trees. They were not very tall but good and wriggly, offering many hand and footholds for climbing. He and Luke spent a lot of time up in the trees, talking about stuff.

By the time Luke had caught up and hauled himself onto a sturdy branch beside his brother, Gideon was leaning over and peering hard into the garden which backed on to Annie's at the bottom fence. 'Ssshh! Listen!' he said to Luke, rather unnecessarily. All Luke ever did was *shhh* and *listen*.

Luke raised an ironic eyebrow, but cocked his head and listened slightly harder.

Someone was crying.

'Sounds like a little kid,' said Gideon. He edged further along his branch, squinting down through the lush green leaves all around them, until he could see past the top of the wooden plank fence into the garden below. And now he saw the source of the crying.

Below him a small boy was hanging.

'Hey! You all right?' he called and the boy twisted his head up. He was about five or six, Gideon reckoned, with pale red hair, freckles and eyes puffed up from crying. He was wearing dungarees and a blue T-shirt—and he was dangling by one denim shoulder strap from the branch of a tree a short distance from the fence.

'I got stuck,' sniffed the boy. 'I can't get down.'

'Don't worry, we'll get you down,' said Gideon, easing himself further along the branch, which drooped alarmingly over the fence. He swung himself across it and then let go, landing with a thud on the soft grass below. 'Luke—might need your help!' he called back and a few seconds later Luke thudded down next to him.

'If you grab his feet and pull him down a bit, I can probably reach the shoulder strap and undo it,' said Gideon.

'I was gonna undo it,' gulped the boy. 'But it was a big drop.' He wiped his small face furiously with grubby hands, trying hard not to cry again.

'You're right. It is a big drop,' said Gideon. 'It was a good thing you didn't undo it.' He glanced along the rather overgrown back garden and saw a red brick house. It wasn't a very big garden. 'Didn't you call for your mum?' he asked as Luke gently pulled the boy's feet and then grabbed his knees, bending the thick branch down far enough for Gideon to reach the snagged denim strap and undo the button on it.

'She's not—' The boy stopped himself and bit on his lip. 'She couldn't hear me,' he said.

'Well, we can take you in to her, and she can give you a drink of squash or something,' said Gideon, undoing the button. The freed branch pinged back upwards immediately and he helped Luke catch the boy and put him on the ground. As the kid's dungarees scrunched up Gideon noticed his pudgy legs were a mottled blue, as if he'd been suspended up there a long time and his blood circulation was messed up. 'How'd you get all caught up like that?'

'I was climbing the tree,' said the boy, rubbing his ankles. 'And I felled off.'

'Well, you're OK now! Let's take you in to your mum,' said Gideon, grabbing the kid's hand.

The boy walked a few unsteady steps back down the garden with them and then pulled his hand out of Gideon's. 'It's OK,' he said. 'I can go now.' He moved on alone, his hands bunched up tightly in fists. 'Thanks,' he said, over his shoulder. 'Bye.'

Luke touched Gideon's arm. He was looking closely at the house.

'What?' said Gideon.

Luke looked at him and signed, *Something's wrong*.

'What? With that kid?' Gideon squinted after the boy as he disappeared into a side passage.

Luke shook his head.

'You think he's a mini burglar or something?' Gideon grinned. 'Should we call in Special Toddler Squad?'

It's the house, signed Luke. *Windows shut. Like there's nobody in it.*

They heard the clunk of a door from the side passage. Luke moved across the garden towards

34

it. He signed back to Gideon, who was making perplexed noises. *We can't get back up over the fence anyway—our tree branches have sprung up too high to climb back. We have to go out the front and walk back around the roads.*

The side passage was dark and cool and a white painted door with wobbly glass in the top half was shut, but not locked. Luke opened it and stepped inside. The house *smelt* lived in. He could see, as he arrived in a small kitchen, that someone had recently had some soup and bread here. The saucepan lay in the sink, soaking, and half a loaf was in a bag on a wood effect work surface. Other crockery sat unwashed on the draining board and a pile of clothes was draped over an ironing board. It was messy—definitely used. So why did he have a sense of someone . . . missing?

'*Luke!* We can't just come in uninvited,' hissed Gideon, who'd just come in, uninvited.

Call hello, signed Luke.

Gideon sighed. For a boy who couldn't speak, Luke could be remarkably bossy. 'Hello! Anyone here?' he called out. In response there was a thud and a scuffle in the hallway. 'Hey, kid!' he went on. 'We just wanted to check you were OK.'

35

He and Luke stepped into the green carpeted hallway just in time to see the under-stairs cupboard door apparently pull itself shut. Gideon knelt next to it and knocked on the varnished pine. 'Hey— don't be scared. What's up? Where's your mum?'

'Go away!' came a muffled response.

Gideon shrugged at Luke. Luke turned and went to check the other rooms of the house, unable to shake the prickly sensation that something was amiss here. The sitting room held two squashy old leather sofas, an electric fire, switched off, and a TV which was on with the sound turned down. Toys were laid out in one part of the carpet as if the kid had been playing a game, but otherwise it was fairly tidy. The dining room was dominated by a table covered in bits of rock and fossil. Upstairs were three bedrooms, the middle sized one obviously the boy's: Spiderman posters on the wall and toys underfoot. The other two rooms looked like a daughter's room and a parent's room. The parent's room was very tidy. He checked the bathroom too, for thoroughness, but he knew it was empty. And it was. The kid was home alone.

'My mum's coming back!' the kid was shouting as Luke went back downstairs. Gideon was peering through a gap in the under-stairs cupboard door. 'Go away!'

'I don't want to scare him by dragging him out of it,' he said to Luke. 'Where's his mum, eh? Maybe she just popped out to the shops or something?'

Luke shook his head. *You should go and ask the neighbours,* he signed.

'OK,' said Gideon. 'You wait here then and try to calm him down.'

How, exactly?

'I dunno . . . tap the door comfortingly.' Gideon ignored the rude remark his brother was signing at him and opened the front door. He didn't get past the threshold. Someone hit him in the face and knocked him flat on his back.

4

'I'VE ALREADY CALLED THE POLICE! They're already coming! MATTHEW! MATTY! Are you *all right*? If you've HURT my BROTHER—'

'GAAAH!' responded Gideon. His attacker was kneeling on his chest, hands planted heavily across his face, staring around the hallway. Somewhere outside a dog was barking furiously.

'LYDDY! I'm in HERE!' squeaked the boy from under the stairs. 'I HIDED!'

But Lyddy was no longer paying attention to her brother's situation. She was gaping in astonishment at Luke, who was standing next to the under-stairs cupboard door and tilting his head to one side, eyes similarly wide and mouth comparably open.

'*YOU!*' gasped the girl. And then she dropped her gaze to Gideon, squirming under her hands and knees and making affronted noises. 'And *YOU*!' She slid off him onto the hallway carpet and then stood up hurriedly. 'What are you doing here? In our house? What's going on?'

Gideon sat up, rubbing his cheekbone and nose which had taken the full brunt of this energetic girl's fist not thirty seconds before. 'Well that's some appreciation for a life saving!' he muttered. Because it was the girl from the beach—the girl he'd hurled himself at only that morning. Although less damagingly.

'Lyddy!' The boy's face finally emerged from the cupboard. 'They rescued me from the tree. I got stuck. I think they're goodies. Not baddies.'

She rubbed her hands on her shorts—still as grubby as they had been that morning—and, taking a deep breath, held one out to help Gideon to his feet. 'I'm sorry,' she said. 'I didn't mean to hurt you. I just . . . I was scared. There were people in my house and I knew Matty was in here and I . . . I was scared. OK?'

'We've got to stop meeting like this,' winced Gideon.

She grinned and her face was transformed. 'I know. I agree,' she said. 'How come you had to rescue yet another member of the Carr family, then?'

The boy—Matthew—came and wrapped his hands around her arm. 'I was stuck in the tree,' he said. 'They came over the fence and got me down. But then they came in and I hided. Like you said.'

She rubbed his head and said, 'Good boy. Why don't you go and get Fish in, Matty? He's tied to the gate. Bring him in and I'll do tea soon.' Matty went out to Fish and then it was just the three of them, staring at each other.

'Well,' said Gideon. 'This is nice.'

She regarded them both for a few seconds and then shrugged off the leather satchel they'd first seen her wearing that morning and hung it over the newel post of the stairs. Luke and Gideon could see her scrapes and bruises from the landslip adventure had not been attended to. Smears of dark blood and clumps of gritty sand still decorated her tanned legs and arms. She had obviously only just got back.

'Did you go back to collecting fossils?' asked Gideon. 'Even though we said it was dangerous?'

'Of course not,' she said, leading them back into

the kitchen. 'I'm not an idiot. I had to get to the shop, though, and sell what I had. Sorry, I didn't mean to lie about living at the other side of the beach, but I didn't want to seem rude. I thought your uncle might try to make me go home . . . offer me a lift or something . . . and I had to get to the shop first.'

She filled the kettle at the tap and then set it to boil. 'Would you like a cup of tea?' she asked.

They both nodded, fascinated by the grace with which she moved around the kitchen. As if she owned it. In spite of her earlier agitation she seemed almost regally composed now.

'So, how come your little brother was here on his own?' asked Gideon. He noticed Lydia's shoulders stiffen as she rooted through a cupboard and retrieved teabags.

'Mum must have gone up the shop,' she said. 'She'll be back any minute I expect. It's my fault, really, I should have been back an hour ago. She knew I'd be along any time, so she wouldn't worry about Matty being on his own too long.'

'What about your dad?' asked Gideon. 'Is he at work?'

'Dad's dead.' She said it without emotion as she

41

dunked teabags into their mugs and went to the fridge.

'Oh. I'm sorry,' said Gideon. He didn't know what else to say, so he added, 'Our mum's dead.'

She glanced at them both as she set the milk down next to the boiling kettle. 'Well then, we all know what it's like—so we don't have to talk about it, do we?'

'Agreed,' said Gideon. And he did agree. Their mother, a single parent, had died when they were newborn babies. They didn't remember her and dealing with people's surprise and sympathy got quite wearing, if he was honest. Gideon had ended up with his natural father and Luke, separated in a mistake which their father had not known about until two years ago, had been adopted by Annie.

They drank tea in the small dining room, peering at Lydia's fossil collection spread out across the table on newspaper, while Matthew played with Fish in the sitting room.

'Nice!' said Gideon, prodding at a small ribbed chunk of grey ammonite. 'We nearly got a giant one of these out of the cliff . . . but it was too high up.' There were sharks' teeth too, some squiggly five-pointed star things pressed flat into ancient clay rocks which Lydia said were called 'brittlestars' and some smooth grey bullet-shaped pieces which were, apparently, 'belemnites'. 'So—do you get good money for these?' asked Gideon.

'Sometimes,' she said. 'Depends. These need a bit of work. Some cleaning up. I'll get more for them that way.'

'Are you saving up for something?'

'Sort of,' she said. 'So—do you live with your uncle over there?' She pointed to the fence at the far end of the garden.

'No—we're just staying for a while. Luke's mum lives there.' She wrinkled her brow, confused, so he went on, 'We were separated when we were babies and Luke got adopted. We only met again a couple of years back and now we go to boarding school together and we sometimes stay with our dad or with Luke's adoptive mum. Our uncle takes us out because Luke's mum's a bit disabled. Geddit?'

'O-K,' she smiled, shaking her head. 'I thought *my* life was complicated.'

'We'd better get back,' said Gideon, suddenly remembering that they were supposed to be in the back garden. A stab of panic reminded him that they were chipped and tracked and at any time Jem could show up, furious, and decide to get them helicoptered back to Fenton Lodge for breaking the rules. 'We'll have to run back round the roads, Luke,' he said, and Luke nodded grimly, looking at his watch. They'd been out of the garden for twenty minutes now.

'No you won't,' said Lydia. 'Just go back over the fence. There's a stepladder in the shed.' She took them outside and they wrestled an old aluminium set of steps out of a crowded wooden shed and carried it back up the garden.

'Maybe you and Matty can come over into *our* garden some time this week, eh?' said Gideon as they held the steps steady for Luke to clamber up and over.

'Maybe,' she said, smiling but not committing.

'Well—you know—ask your mum,' said Gideon. 'And then just pop over. We're usually there after tea.'

'I will,' she said, smiling harder and holding steady as Gideon climbed. 'Thanks again . . . and sorry . . . again. Oh—that sounds like Mum back now. Got to go. Byeee.'

As soon as he thumped down on their side of the fence, Gideon beamed at Luke. 'Now she . . . ' he said, ' . . . even messed up and scabby . . . is *very* nice!'

Yes, signed back Luke. *And she's lying.*

Jem felt suddenly prickly. He scanned the gadgetry across the small dressing table and saw the red dots which represented his assets—Gideon and Luke—still within the vicinity of the house. Moving gradually closer to it. His muscles relaxed again, but not totally. He stood and wandered from one side of the small ground floor annexe to the other— there were windows on both front and back walls, which is why he'd chosen to stay in here. He peered into the garden and saw the familiar fluffy blond head of Gideon emerge from a rhododendron bush, the dark spikes of his brother's dyed hair bobbing close behind. The brothers were deep in conversation, Gideon talking back over his shoulder and then twisting round to watch his brother's response. It made Jem smile. It was so instinctive and humorous, even with the barrier of no verbal language on one side. He knew he shouldn't, but he'd got fond of the twins very quickly. It was a good thing this assignment was a short one. Caring too much about the assets clouded your thinking.

He turned back to *mission control* on the dressing table. Two sleek laptops sat open amid a zoo of cutting edge tracking and communications gadgets. On one screen were the feeds from twelve different cameras positioned around the cottage and along the main access roads for a half mile on either side of their location. Minutes earlier he'd watched the brothers climb up into one of the trees at the far end of the garden on one of the screens. They were not easy to see in the branches but the tracker chips showed their location well enough. On the other laptop was a live link satellite view of the same territory. Control oversaw this information constantly from the remote HQ in London, and Bill and Clara had a similar set-up in their holiday let across the road. The three operatives had a shift pattern in place to ensure the camera feeds were monitored around the clock.

Here at the cottage was fairly straightforward. Every neighbour in the road had been discreetly checked out in the weeks before their arrival—and again, two days before it, to be sure there were no new people in the vicinity. No—here was OK. It was when they were all on the move that it turned tricky. Not that he seriously believed anyone was watching. It had been over a year since the attempt to abduct the Colas from a container ship in the North Sea had been thwarted by Owen Hind and his men. The traitors at Fenton Lodge had been hunted down and were either dead or incarcerated for life. The rogue Cola child who'd led to such a horrific breakdown of security and trust was also dead and giving no more information to the French or any other power which might seek to acquire a Cola and a Cola's phenomenal power.

But it was a mistake to assume that anyone had forgotten what Britain had. A secret auction had taken place across the globe before the Colas were rescued, with several countries bidding for them (even if none of them admitted to it). The truth was out there—even if not every significant world power believed it yet. Colas were the most exciting asset on the planet—capable of truly astonishing paranormal feats. Imagine—*kids* who could move things around just by directing their thoughts. Kids who could create perfect and unshakeable illusions. Kids who could heal broken bones with a touch, turn invisible, speak to the dead, find lost things anywhere on the planet—even shapeshift and fly!

The potential was dizzying. So was the threat.

Not for the first time, Jem sighed as he wondered what the future held for these kids. Were they gifted or just cursed? Certainly they could never hope for a normal life.

A movement caught his eye. He glanced up through the window which gave onto the short front garden filled with hydrangea bushes and rows of fuschia shrubs. No. Nothing there. Just the cat. But still his senses prickled. Jem would never admit out loud that he believed in extrasensory perception. Meeting the Colas had forced him to rethink a lot of his ideas, of course. But he had *always* believed in a soldier's ESP. Working as a team in battle forced soldiers to develop their own sixth sense—their survival depended on it. So he never shrugged off a prickle in his senses.

He picked up the secure phone and rang Clara. 'Everything OK?' he said, as soon as she picked up.

There was hesitation on the line. 'Erm . . . actually Bill's throwing his guts up,' came back Clara.

'What?'

'He's been hugging the toilet for the last half hour. Must have eaten a dodgy hotdog from that stand at the beach. I told him not to. The geezer running it looked weird.'

Jem cursed. 'How bad is he?'

There was a pause as Clara checked in on her partner. 'He looks pretty grim,' came back her voice, hollow in the tiled bathroom. 'Yuck. Better not give that bug to me, Bill.' Bill rumbled something unintelligible back at her.

'He says it's malaria,' she snorted. 'He got bitten by something on the beach.'

'Did he?'

'Well, he's got a big itchy bump on his leg. I *really* don't think the two are related!'

'Well, if he's not improved in an hour we'll have to get him replaced,' said Jem.

'Roger *that*!' agreed Clara. 'I'm not nursemaiding pukey boy all night long.'

'Touching concern,' grinned Jem. Clara made him laugh too. For a 27-year-old woman she had a knack of sounding just like a 14-year-old boy. He hung up and sat back down at the dressing table, maximizing each feed one by one before returning to a mosaic view of all twelve cameras. Everything looked normal. So why the prickles?

Checking that his weapon was in its holster

under his jacket he did a circuit of the house and grounds and found nothing amiss. Nothing to cause concern.

'Just Bill's belly,' he told himself .'You're turning into such a worrier.'

5

'So what do you think she's lying about?' asked Gideon as he and Luke plonked themselves down on the elderly swings and creaked to and fro in the late afternoon sun.

Wreeek-aaaw . . . *Wreeek-aaaw* . . . Only the swings spoke for some while as Luke squinted into the middle distance. Then he signed: *It's to do with her mum. She said her mum was just getting back as we went over the fence—but she wasn't. There IS no mum. There hasn't been a mum there for ages.*

'How do you know that?' asked Gideon. 'She might have been out. I mean—they don't look all starving and neglected, do they? Even the dog looks well looked after.'

I didn't say they were neglected, signed Luke, with a huff of frustration. *And they're not. Lydia's doing it all—can't you see? She's being the mum.*

Gideon peered back down the garden, gnawing on his lower lip. Certain things began to make sense to him now. How the kid had been stuck up the tree for so long for one thing . . . and how he hadn't called for help. He knew there *was* no help from the house. No mum.

The mum's bedroom was totally neat and tidy . . . like a hotel room, Luke went on. *Like it's ready for when she comes back . . . But Lydia's room, and Matthew's room— all messed up like normal kids' rooms. And remember after the landslip, how desperate she was to get her bag back? All her fossils and tools?* Gideon nodded. *Well, she said to Jem that she* had *to have them. She said 'They're all I have to make our money. 'Not 'my money' like any other normal self-obsessed teenager—'OUR money.' I bet you I'm right. She's selling fossils to buy food. There is NO mum.*

'Whoa,' murmured Gideon, feeling a strange constriction around his chest. He realized it was sympathy. And an odd streak of protectiveness, even though she was in no way *his* responsibility. 'How is she keeping it together? I'd *freak* if I got left on my own with a kid to look after. What's happened to her mum?'

Luke shrugged. *I don't know—but if it gets out*

52

they're on their own they'll both end up in care, won't they? That's why she was funny with Jem.

Gideon shook his head, frustrated. 'What do you *mean*, funny with Jem?'

She wanted to steer clear of him. She wasn't really worried about being offered a lift home when she wanted to go off and sell her fossils first. She was worried he might find out about her secret and call in social services.

Gideon shook his head again. 'How do you pick all this up?'

Luke grinned. *I WATCH people. I LISTEN. I notice their behaviour. You're too busy larking about . . .*

'Oh well . . . with you and Dax and Lisa and Mia all being so super sensitive around me, why would I need to bother?' It was true, Gideon knew, that he was a bit of a dunce on the ESP front. He could lift a transit van six feet into the air—no hands!—but he couldn't pick up those little emotional clues all the others did quite so easily. Although, like many twins, he had an instinct for Luke's thoughts, for everyone else he tended to need subtitles. 'So what are we going to do?' he added, furrowing his brow.

Luke shrugged again and signed: *Nothing.*

Nothing? Gideon signed back, more violently.

Why should we do anything? She's coping fine, isn't she?

'We should tell her we know,' said Gideon. 'See if she wants any help.'

She'll freak out, warned Luke. *She really DOESN'T want you to know.*

'We could help out with money,' said Gideon, swinging harder as enthusiasm built up inside him for a whole new rescue. 'We've got quite a bit in our Cola accounts now, haven't we?'

You could try—but I bet she wouldn't take it, signed Luke. *MAJOR pride going on in that one. It's one of the reasons you fancy her.*

'Well, I'm going to try anyway,' said Gideon, jumping off the swing at the highest point and landing with a thud on the lawn. 'We're only here a week and then we'll be gone. If I can get some cash out without Jem getting suspicious, I reckon I could get her to take it. Maybe just post it in an envelope anonymously.'

Whatever, Romeo. Luke was chuckling with quiet clicks and rasps. *We could ask Jem to stop on the way to the castle tomorrow and take us to a cashpoint. Better think up something expensive you want to buy . . .*

Bill had been replaced. He'd vomited himself

dry and around 10 p.m. the previous evening a car from Control had arrived, looking like a taxi. It had dropped off the new guy, John Farrier, before taking Bill away, waxy white, clutching a hot water bottle to his knotted insides and sipping kaolin and morphine mixture from the bottle. It made Jem uneasy because he'd not worked with Farrier before, but the man—a wiry character with receding brown hair, a small mouth, and hard grey eyes—seemed steady enough. Control told him they were confident of Farrier's abilities. He'd acquitted himself in the field many times. And Clara was happy to be relieved of Bill and his stomach bug. The new 'couple' were three cars behind them now as they crossed the Island bound for Carisbrooke Castle.

'Jem—can we stop at a cashpoint?' Gideon bobbed up and down in the seat behind like an excited puppy. 'I've hardly got any money left!'

'I can sub you for the castle gift shop,' said Jem.

'Thanks . . . but, they've got these, like trebuchets and maces and swords and stuff . . . and me and Luke want to get some and do a big battle re-enactment thing in the back garden and that'll cost loads . . . and we've got money in our accounts.'

'It's OK. You can owe me,' said Jem, changing gear and overtaking a tractor on the long country road.

'We . . . we just want to use our cards,' said Gideon forlornly, waving his little purple cashpoint card. 'We hardly *ever* get to use these—you know that. It's . . . kind of fun. We just want to have a go . . . See if the PIN works . . . '

Jem shook his head but he smiled. 'So—all the Island's attractions on offer to you and all you really want is to play with a cashpoint.'

'Can we?' grinned Gideon and Luke mirrored his keen expression.

'OK, if you must,' sighed Jem and he drove left into the town as soon as the country lane joined the main ring road.

Gideon took out £200—his limit. He knew there would be questions later, but for now Jem wasn't paying attention. He was checking out the road and pavement around them, as ever, on constant alert along with the two other operatives who were never more than half a street away.

Gideon gave half the cash to Luke for safekeeping and carefully pocketed the rest. He had, in fact, got a few quid in his pocket anyway, and this was what he planned to spend in the castle gift shop, to allay any suspicions that Jem might have.

The castle was quiet when they arrived mid morning. It was a Monday in term time and there were no holidaying children or school parties in evidence, just a handful of older people roaming contentedly around the well-tended grounds and lawns. Gideon and Luke wandered along pale sandstone battlements, gazing sometimes out at the view of the rolling island hills all around them and then back across the keep and the formal Edwardian garden and the assorted dwellings built within the walls. It was a pretty castle and strangely welcoming, despite its sometimes gruesome history, with crenellated battlements worn smooth by time and softened by yellow lichen. Its medieval motte stood high on an almost conical hill in one corner. The great hall and the chapel had red tiled pitch roofs and high mullioned windows which glinted in the morning light. Rooks called in their high cracked voices from the trees within the walls and donkeys occasionally brayed in their stables.

'Ooh—the donkey wheel thingy is going to go off in a minute,' said Gideon, turning to Jem who was wandering a few paces behind them, taking in the views in a such a relaxed way that you'd never guess he could chuck three highly trained attackers over the battlements in less than six seconds without breaking a sweat if he so chose—all while keeping up a running commentary to Control via his earpiece.

'Donkey on a wheel?' echoed Jem, smiling. 'Can't miss *that* can we?'

They hurried down the steps, holding fast to wooden handrails, and arrived at the small well house in the centre of the castle grounds in time to see the donkey being led in by a woman with a ponytail and a cheerful smile. Inside the cool stone building were old oak workings designed to pull water up from a deep, deep well, aided by a donkey walking the wooden wheel they were attached to. As the donkey—called Jigsaw, his keeper informed the small crowd of a dozen or so people—shuffled behind the wheel and then stepped onto it, there was a small quacking noise from Gideon's jeans pocket, interrupting the guide's explanation of the donkey wheel's history.

Jem scowled and a few people sniggered. Gideon hauled his mobile phone out, feeling hot around the ears, and quickly muted it. He could see a text message flaring across the small screen. *Call me now!* It was from Lisa, back at Fenton Lodge. Typical Lisa. Gideon edged back a little, behind Luke, while the guide continued her talk and the donkey began to clop along, turning the great oak wheel and the workings connected to it. Quickly Gideon palmed his phone and with one thumb texted *What?* In response he got *Call me NOW!* Gideon gritted his teeth, vaguely aware of a tickling feeling across his scalp. He texted back **Can't!** and then got another a few seconds later saying *DON'T LEAVE THE WELL HOUSE!*

Gideon felt a chill run across his neck and shoulders. Lisa was several counties north and she *knew* where they were right at this moment. He was well aware that she was a dowser . . . someone who could locate people many miles away with some supernatural part of her brain. She could also read minds, when she chose to (which she rarely did), as well as talk to spirits and communicate telepathically with certain people (not him). Gideon had known Lisa for more than three years, but her talents never stopped giving him goosepimples—or a tickling scalp while she was dowsing him. Why did she want him to stay put in the well house? He had no idea.

He thumbed back **OK. BUT WHY?** and sent.

Call me from the well house ASAP, she texted back.

The short talk was coming to an end—he'd missed most of it and Luke was nudging him, warning him that Jem, across the other side of the round stone wall of the well, was getting annoyed about the phone twiddling. Gideon put the phone back in his pocket and concentrated as best he could while the guide finished her patter with a demonstration involving a water jug.

'This will give you an idea how deep this well is,' she explained, tipping water from the jug through the iron grating which stretched across the dark round yawn of stone. The water splashed a little on the ironwork and then there was silence for a few seconds. The water was clearly falling a long, long way. Then, a tiny distant splash echoed back up to them. There were murmurs of wonder and finally the crowd began to move out of the well house and on to the next attraction. Gideon stayed put and Luke loitered with him. *What?* he signed. With Jem's view briefly blocked by the exiting visitors, Gideon signed back: *A message from Lisa. She wants us to stay in here. I don't know why!*

A few seconds later, as the guide led the donkey away, his muted phone vibrated in his pocket and Gideon snatched it up to his ear. 'Hi, Lisa,' he said, careful to keep the anxiety out of his voice while Jem was watching. 'What's up?'

'Look down the well,' said Lisa.

'Yeah, we're in the well house at Carisbrooke Castle,' said Gideon, as if Lisa was a normal person, just asking what he was doing.

'Are you looking down the well?' snapped Lisa and Gideon could picture her flipping back her long blonde hair and rolling her dark blue eyes with impatience.

'Yeah—looking right down the well now,' he replied. 'Luke and Uncle Jem too. It's forty-nine metres deep—did you know that?'

'Touch the metal grating,' instructed Lisa.

'Why's that then?' Gideon queried, keeping his tone light despite the knot of tension inside him. Whatever was going on, there was no way he was going to risk spooking Jem. Not after yesterday. Or they'd be back with Lisa at Fenton Lodge in time for tea.

'Something's coming through. Something important. Elizabeth is trying to tell me something but it's all too faint. If you touch the grating we'll make better contact.'

'What?' Gideon couldn't help squawking. 'How does that help?'

'Just do it!'

Luke had walked round to Jem and was distracting him by asking to borrow his binoculars so he could peer down into the well with them. The well had lights placed deep down inside, so there was some point to this. The main point, though, was that Luke was keeping some of Jem's focus off Gideon. Gideon reached into the well and grasped the cold, slightly wet grille of iron. At once a chilly tingle shot up his arm and he let go.

'NO! Don't let go!' yelled Lisa. 'Hold it again, you wuss. It's only a bit of spirit energy. Elizabeth! Yes. Result!' There was silence for a few seconds as Gideon hooked his fingers through the grating. He felt as if he'd stuck his hand into a freezer and the hairs on his arm all stood to attention, goosepimples rising up beneath them. He got the distinct impression that something was looking up at him from the inky black water so far below.

'Who's this then?' he prompted, with a gulp.

'Elizabeth? A friend of yours?'

'Elizabeth Ruffin. Drowned in the well,' said Lisa, impatiently, clearly trying to concentrate on her conversation with the woman's spirit. 'Now sshhh . . . wait a minute.'

'Why are you clutching the grating, Gideon?' asked Jem. His tone was reasonable, mildly amused. Gideon decided lying was pointless.

'Oh, it's just Lisa,' he said, shrugging. 'She's on some ghost hunt lark and wanted me to touch this well and see if I could channel some drowned old biddy back to her. Mediums, eh? Cuh! But you know what Lisa's like . . . '

Jem raised an eyebrow. Fortunately he *didn't* know what Lisa was like. Lisa was the last medium in the world to ever seek out a spirit just for fun. The words 'ghost hunt lark' were not even in her vocabulary. She had more spirit action than she could handle—or would have if she didn't know how to shut some of it out. She certainly never went looking for it. Which was one of the reasons why Gideon was feeling so shivery—along with channelling a ghost, of course. Lisa would never be doing this without a reason. A *serious* reason.

Just as Jem was walking round to him, ready to

intervene, Lisa said. 'It's OK. Let go. I've got the message now.'

Gideon let go of the grating with relief and stood away from the well. 'So we can leave the well house now?' he said, adding sarcasm to his voice to hide the nerves.

'Yes,' she said. 'But don't go in the g—'

Snap.

The call was abruptly cut off as Jem took the phone. 'Enough chatting with the girlfriend, Gid,' he said. He was uncomfortable with the Colas carrying mobile phones. He felt they were too easy for enemies to hack into or to use as a tracking device. Paulina Sartre, the principal of Fenton Lodge, had insisted they carry phones, however. Her argument was that Colas, like any other teenagers, could encounter everyday mishaps and problems, the kind that did not require an emergency stampede of special operatives. For these she felt they should have mobile phones like normal people.

'She's not my girlfriend,' said Gideon, wincing. 'Why did you cut us off? She was just about to tell me what the ghost said!'

'*Ghost,*' muttered Jem, shaking his head. He put the phone back in Gideon's hand, though. 'Come on—let's go and see the Great Hall.'

'Can I just go to the toilet?' said Gideon, anxious to get away and call Lisa back.

'Phone,' said Jem, holding out his hand. 'I'm not waiting out here for half an hour while you gossip.'

Gideon sighed and handed it over while Luke sat down with Jem to wait for his return from the low brick toilet block. Luke flopped back down on the grass, throwing his arms behind his head and there was a little thud on Gideon's foot. Luke had quietly thrown him his own phone (he could only use it for texting but still found that useful). Gideon grinned and scooped it up, glad that a cacophony of rook calls had disguised the sound of the phone landing.

'What?' he said as soon as Lisa picked up.

'Elizabeth Ruffin was telling me some stuff. And . . . another Elizabeth was backing her up. That place is teeming with tragic Lizzies,' said Lisa. 'Anyway . . . here's the message. *The dark twin has death for you.*'

'The dark twin?' Gideon glanced out of the window above the sinks at Luke, his black hair wafting about in the breeze as he sat next to Jem. 'What—Luke? Don't be daft.'

'Look—it might be Luke, it might not,' she said. 'I mean—probably not. I don't think Luke's got it in for anyone, although with all that silent brooding, who knows?' She was being flippant. 'No . . . I mean it might be to do with him . . . but the message isn't for you anyway.'

'Well . . . who *is* it for? The *donkey*?'

'It's for someone called Jeremiah. And it's . . . *serious,* Gid. It's . . . blue.'

'Blue?'

'Yeah . . . I kind of get colours in my head with some of them and one thing I've noticed over the years is . . . the blue ones are always the worst. Serious. So you'd better find this Jeremiah bloke and get him out of the castle. Particularly the Great Hall.'

Gideon gulped. 'OK,' he said. 'Anything else?'

'Nope. That's all you need to know. Be glad you don't have to put up with all the whingeing and wheezing too.'

'Whingeing and wheezing?'

'Yeah. The younger Elizabeth. Daughter of King Charles I. Died of a nasty chill in one of the bedrooms. She's still really narked about it. Oh GREAT, now they're all coming in. Charley boy too.

It's a great big dead royal bleedin' knees up . . . '

'OK, have fun,' said Gideon, noticing Jem now standing up and moving towards the toilet block, and Clara and the new guy peering down at him through a camera lens from the battlements. They were getting twitchy. 'Gotta go.'

He emerged from the toilet shaking water off his hands. 'Air drier's not working,' he grinned at Jem. 'So where next?'

'Great Hall,' said Jem. 'Artefacts and suchlike.'

Gideon followed him a few steps, pondering something. There was only one way to be sure. 'Jeremiah . . . ?' he said.

Jem turned round immediately and narrowed his eyes at him. 'What did you call me?' he asked.

'Is that your name then?' grinned Gideon. 'I was just larking about . . . but . . . yeah . . . it is your name, isn't it? I can tell by the look on your face. Not Jeremy. Jeremiah.'

'You do know I can kill you with a single blow, don't you?' muttered Jem, inclining his head and raising his dark eyebrows. 'And anyway, it's Uncle Jem to you. Don't forget it.'

Gideon grinned some more, although he was actually beginning to feel distinctly rattled. He had been hoping Lisa's spirit message had been for some random old bloke in the castle that day. He'd hoped to call out the name in the Great Hall and see who turned his head and then say there was an urgent message in the gift shop or something and see the man toddle off away from whatever danger awaited him. Then Gideon could feel good for doing his bit and forget it.

But no. It was Jem. *Their* Jem. And, apparently, a dark twin had death for him.

He sidled up next to Luke and muttered to him as he handed back his phone. 'You're not planning on killing Jem, are you?'

Luke snorted with amusement and then signed back, *As if I COULD! No—what's up? What's Lisa getting her knickers in a twist about?*

Gideon stared at the back of Jem's head. He couldn't really take this seriously, could he? Lisa had been right before . . . but she'd also been wrong. And who was going to attack Jem in the middle of a tourist attraction with two other special ops just a twenty second dash away? Nobody.

And if he tried to warn Jem—what then? The helicopter. No doubt about it.

She thinks someone's out to get Jem, he signed back. *A 'dark twin'.*

Helpful as ever then, signed back Luke, grinning. Lisa's messages were often obscure. *We'd better keep a look out then, hadn't we? And if I look like going for him, just stop me, OK?*

It turned out the Great Hall was empty anyway, apart from an elderly volunteer guide at a desk who didn't look capable of bringing death to a passing ant. A dark twin of death wasn't coming to Jem here. 'Blue' message or not, Lisa was just off on a flight of fancy, thought Gideon. Probably needed to eat some sugar or something. Clara and the new bloke had come in behind them now too and that made him feel better still.

Jem turned back and watched his charges wandering around the Great Hall, peering into the display cases and playing with the old stringed wooden instruments on a stand. As Gideon began to twang a tune on the zither Jem allowed himself a chuckle and a smile.

And the man training a sniper gun on him from a cavity in the high ceiling paused, his finger caressing the trigger. Smiled. And changed his mind.

6

Lydia took Matty with her after school. She felt bad about it. He'd already had to wait twenty minutes in the playground for her to run out of her school and get home and back to his to collect him. Usually he was the last kid waiting and sometimes the mothers heading away from the gates would give her looks as if to wonder what she was thinking of, leaving a reception-year kid waiting alone. Worse, they would sometimes ask after her mother and she'd have to lie. So far it had worked but she didn't know how much longer she could go on about agoraphobia before someone got 'helpful' and sent a social worker along to their house.

Poor Matty was going to have to walk a long way, too, and he already looked tired after a day at school. Every time she collected him her belly would knot up, expecting this to be the day that he'd given the game away and told a teacher how he had no mummy at home. Only a big sister. *But he WILL have a mummy at home again . . . soon . . . I'm sure of it,* she told herself. Well, it wasn't today, anyway, that their world of lies was due to unravel. Matty's teacher gave her a cheery wave as she closed her classroom window. Cheery and not too interested.

'Hi, Matty,' she said, taking his small pudgy hand. 'How was school today?' She remembered Mum saying that to him and so she reminded herself to ask the same, even though her mind was filled with more pressing concerns. Like whether there would be enough money for this week's food.

'OK,' he said. 'Can I have an ice lolly?' He eyed the corner shop and she sighed and then tugged him in the opposite direction.

'No, Matty. Not enough money.' His lower lip stuck out and she scooped an apple out of her pocket swiftly. 'How about this? Nice and juicy. Good for you.' They had been given a free apple at school today as part of a healthy eating project her year was on. She'd pocketed hers immediately, thinking of just this moment.

71

Matty's lip stuck out a few seconds longer as he took the fruit, but then he shrugged and bit into it.

'Come on. We have to go to the fossil shop,' she said. 'I got some really good fossils at the landslip first thing.'

Although she'd been up late last night, cleaning her latest finds, she'd gone out before dawn, while Matty was still sleeping, and cycled five miles to the beach to plunder its newly revealed cliff face. She'd found ammonites and belemnites and some lovely ancient fish in the clay. She'd cut as much out as she could manage alone, hefted a load of it into her satchel and got back with it by 7.30 a.m., excited but tired. By the time she'd cleaned up and got herself and Matty into school uniform there was only just time to make their lunchtime sandwiches and shove some toast and orange juice into them both before they had to run. Literally. She could *not* be late. There might be a phone call home if she was and then . . . questions about why no mother ever answered or called back. For the same reason she had to do all her homework and get it in on time. She had never worked so hard in her life. Fossil collecting and cleaning and selling to the shop, looking after Matty, cooking and cleaning and homework ruled her life. She rarely watched TV. By the time they'd eaten and she'd bathed Matty and got him to bed (and read a story like Mum used to) there was homework or fossil cleaning and then bed where she slept like the dead before getting up at dawn.

During the week, her best fossil hunting time was before Matty woke up. She dreaded Matty waking when she wasn't there. That would be awful; but so far, if he had woken, he had not noticed he was alone. She left a big message stuck to the front door, reading *MATTY! Don't worry. I'm out getting fossils and I will be back by this time:* And then she would draw a clock face with seven thirty marked clearly on it, like the clock in his telling-the-time book, and the one in the kitchen. It was a very good thing he was a bright little boy who could read well already.

It seemed more OK to leave him for a couple of hours on a Saturday or Sunday, because he could watch TV and play with toys for hours without really noticing she wasn't there. And she had the phone. The cheap little Pay As You Go phone. She hardly ever used it. Just three or four times over the weekend to make sure Matty was OK. And she had trained him to hit the Lyddy button on their phone in the hallway whenever he wanted to. It was easy for him to do and got him straight through to her on the pre-programmed number. And it got paid for automatically on direct debit.

'Can we go on the bus?' asked Matty, through a mouthful of apple. She grimaced. She really wanted to catch the bus. But there just wasn't enough money. Maybe, though, they could go part of the way . . . She jingled through the coins in the outer pocket of the heavy satchel. Yes, they could go halfway with what she had, as long as the driver didn't decide she was over 16. She glanced back down the road and saw the No. 24 coming. The satchel was *so* heavy . . . and she was sure to get good money for what was in it. So . . . what the hell . . .

'OK, Matty. We can go halfway on the bus, all right?' They ran across to the stop and hopped onto the bus a few seconds later. The driver didn't eye her suspiciously like some did these days when she asked for two half fares. She wasn't yet 15 but girls in her own class often got into bars, claiming they were 18. It was hard to tell.

'The back! The back!' squeaked Matty and ran down the aisle, intent on reaching the long bench seat where he could peer out of the rear window and make faces at drivers behind them. She smiled. He was very 'five' and she was pleased about that. She knew *she* was not at all 'fourteen' these days. In fact, she felt more like 34. The same age her mum was. Today. Wherever she was. *Happy birthday, Mum,* she called out, sadly, in her head. Not as sadly as the day she'd sung happy birthday to Matty a few weeks back. That had been awful. If even her little boy's birthday couldn't bring Mum back, what could? Still, she hadn't let it show. She'd made him a little cake and bought him some cheap plastic toy he'd seen on TV, thanking her lucky stars that he was too young to want a computer gadget of some kind just yet.

She *had* to get more money in. She patted the satchel, taking some comfort from it, but it wasn't enough. It never was. And now she was worried about going out again at the weekend. The encounter with Gideon and Luke in the house yesterday had alarmed her horribly. Poor Matty. Stuck up that tree for ages and having to be rescued by strangers. No. She would have to take him with her on the weekend fossil hunts now. It would be a nightmare, of course, because he would keep wandering off. But she'd have to find a way. She had wanted to get him into a weekend play group, but they'd insisted Mum must come along and fill in some forms and she couldn't convince them to let her take a form home for her mother. They didn't go for the agoraphobic line. They at least wanted a phone conversation with Matty's mum and that was no good. She could fake letters and even her mum's signature (she'd spent hours practising) but she couldn't fake a 34-year-old voice.

'Here we go, time to get off,' she said, grabbing Matty's hand ten minutes later. He looked sulky. He knew they were nowhere near the fossil shop. 'Come on,' she chivvied. 'And don't leave your apple core on the seat. Pick it up.'

They jumped off the bus and then followed its retreating shape, losing it over the hill in no time. The rest of the journey would be twenty minutes, if Matty didn't get too whiny and demand to be carried. With the weight in her satchel she just couldn't manage that today. She got him to count yellow and red cars as they walked and—thankfully—this kept him occupied until Adrian's Island Treasures came into view.

'Yo, Lyddy!' called Adrian when he saw her in the doorway. 'You got treasure for me?'

'Yep—worth a fortune,' she promised with a cheerful grin.

'Hello, little man,' Adrian grinned at Matty who grinned back and then went to look at the sharks' teeth while Lydia upended the satchel and carefully allowed her treasure to slide out.

Adrian tipped back the Indiana Jones style hat he liked to wear in the shop (it covered his thinning fair hair and gave him a dinosaur hunter look, he believed) and sorted through Lyddy's finds with grunts of approval and one or two low whistles. 'Nice—a complete one!' He held up a small but beautifully formed ammonite, still embedded in a lump of Wealden clay but obviously undamaged.

'What can you give me?' asked Lydia, cutting to it. She wanted to get home. If this brought in enough they would bus back the whole way.

'We-ell,' said Adrian, tightening his lips and furrowing his brow. 'Business is a bit slow right now . . . '

'It's *not*,' she snapped back. 'You had a crowd in here at the weekend. You were mobbed! Don't give me that.'

'Well, they might have been looking, but they weren't all buying . . . ' he went on, shaking his head.

'Ade. There are *other* fossil shops,' she growled. She knew he was mostly winding her up. Adrian was OK. He paid her a fair price but seemed to think he was obliged to haggle. 'How much?'

He folded his arms and sighed. '£35.'

'Oh come on! That's got to be £150 worth.'

'Yeah—but first I've got to do the cleaning up and that takes time and time is money . . .'

'I've cleaned most of them already. £60! That's fair. You know it.'

'£45. And you're robbing me, Lyd.'

'£55!'

'£50—and only because I know how much you want that new bike,' he said.

'OK. £50.' It was the figure she'd had in her head.

'Surely you must be close to buying it by now,' he said as he opened the till and counted out the notes. 'How much is it?'

'Oh—hundreds and hundreds,' she murmured. She'd fed him the bike line four months ago when Mum had been gone two weeks and she'd first realized she had to earn food money. Luckily all the other household bills, like electricity and water rates, were paid automatically and there must still be enough money in Mum's account to keep them going OK, because she only ever got statements in the post, not big red payment demands. No—it was just the food she needed to pay for. And clothes, soon. Her school uniform was getting embarrassingly short and tight, but she planned to wear it until the end of the summer term anyway. Shoes would be next though. Matty would have to have new ones in September and if Mum wasn't back by then . . . but she would be. She *would* be.

'A penny for them.' Adrian interrupted her thoughts, waving five tenners in her face. 'Well—actually five thousand pennies.'

'Oh—yeah—miles away,' she grinned, wearily. 'Thanks, Ade. That's brilliant. I'll be back in a few days.'

'I'm counting on it,' he smiled. 'You OK? You look . . . knackered. And like you could use a big dinner.'

'You asking me out?' She raised a sceptical eyebrow and he backed away, chuckling and waving his hands.

'My girlfriend would have something to say about that,' he said.

'Come on, Matty!' she called out. 'Back on the bus now.'

'All the way?' he asked, hopefully.

'Yup, all the way.'

The trip back was better. Knowing she could feed them both for a week on her fossil money undid some of the knots in her belly. But not entirely. That last bit would never unknot until Mum was back. The bus stopped on the cliff road above the landslip which had provided her wages. Not close enough to be at risk on the ever-eroding Island cliffs, but close enough to look at the sea. It lay big and blue and shifting restlessly. Through the bus's open windows came the scent of salt and sand from the beach below.

A man was waiting at the stop and he got on board and took up the seat opposite them. They'd had to take one of the side benches this time, as the back seat was occupied. Matty was twisted around, pressing his nose against the glass and steaming it up, but the man glanced at Lydia and gave her a little smile. He was around 30, she thought, lean and fit in jeans and a crisply ironed black shirt, with piercing dark brown eyes. His short dark hair had an odd white streak running through it at his left temple. His hands were restless, drumming on a black holdall which he had placed across his knees and he glanced at her several more times, still smiling. Something about the smiling made her shiver and look away. He seemed . . . unpredictable. As if he might draw a white rabbit from that black holdall at any moment . . . or a flame thrower.

The journey got less comfortable. So much so that she took Matty off a stop early and watched the bus chug on up the hill without them, happy that it would wind around the steep lane and on up to the Shanklin road and take that odd man with it. She, meanwhile, could cut through a little patch of trees and shrubs and get to her house nearly as fast as if she'd waited another stop along the road. She and Matty got there quickly and once inside, she sent her little brother to let Fish into the back garden for a wee and a run around. Before closing the front door she saw an envelope on the mat. A thick brown envelope. It had *Lydia* written on it in unfamiliar handwriting. Nothing else. Putting down her empty satchel in the hallway, she sat down on the front step, its terracotta tiles warm in the June sun, and ripped open the envelope. Her eyes widened when she saw what was in it. A wad of £20 notes. Her heart leapt in her chest and she jumped to her feet, staring all around, in case the deliverer of this package was still nearby, watching. DAMN! Somebody was giving her money! £200, she realized, swiftly thumbing through it. Somebody must KNOW! Damn! Damn! *Damn!*

Be calm. Be *calm,* she instructed herself. *Think.* Who would do this? Who could know? Her next door neighbours? She thought about that. Mrs Crawford on one side was too elderly to get out much and notice Lydia and Matty's situation had in any way changed. And the young couple who rented on the other side only occasionally waved as they went in and out from their car. They'd only lived there a few months and never saw Mum before anyway. No . . . she couldn't imagine any neighbours helping out. Someone at school? No . . . Who else? Some anonymous hero intent on saving them?

'Oh, you've got to be kidding me!' She whacked her forehead and leaned against the door post as the obvious answer came to her. Those two boys. Gideon and Luke. Here in the house with just Matty yesterday. They must have put two and two together and come up—unfortunately—with four. 'Damn!' she said again.

'Damn! Damn! Damn!' shouted Matty, running down the hallway with Fish.

'Matty! Don't say that!'

'*You* did!'

'Well . . . I'm allowed to. You're not.'

'You're not allowed. I'll tell Mum when she comes back.'

Lydia smiled sadly at him. 'OK, Matty-boy. You tell Mum I said naughty words. I won't mind.'

She settled him to watch CBBC and went out into the back garden, the money shoved back in its envelope. The stepladder was still in place below the fence. She would just climb up it to get over the fence and take the money back. She'd take it from the envelope and pin it under a stone on the veranda that overlooked their garden and if it wasn't from Gideon and Luke they would never work out where it came from—and if it was, they would hopefully get the message that she didn't want their help, or their interference. Part of her twinged with the thought of letting the money go. She could stay off the beach at dawn for a month with that much. Get some proper rest and be less tired at school. But no. This was just asking for trouble.

She hitched up her already too short school skirt and clambered up the ladder, the money envelope tucked in her waistband. She would creep up the garden and stay out of sight as long as she could. It looked deserted and she could run from shrub to shrub and hide under those rhododendrons to be sure she was alone before she did the last dash. She got up to the low boughs of the tree and swung into them easily, peering up through a gap in the leaves. And then she froze.

For sitting quietly this side of the closest rhododendron, still grasping his holdall and still smiling, was the man from the bus.

7

Gideon felt uneasy all the way back from the Isle of Wight Zoo. Now that he and Luke had delivered the money his mind was free to wander back to Lisa's warning at the castle that morning. While Annie was putting lunch on the table and chatting to Jem, he had slipped over the fence into Lydia's back garden and scooted round to the front of the house to post it, leaving Luke waiting anxiously on their side of the fence, ready to reassure Jem that they'd just dropped a ball and Gideon was getting it back, if his gadgetry warned him they had wandered too far. They had dropped a ball, too, to be on the safe side.

But the mission was accomplished with ease and after lunch they had all set out to the zoo in Sandown, on the eastern coast, and it was while they were looking at the tigers in their enclosures, that Gideon had begun to think about Lisa's message again. *The dark twin has death for you.* It was, he had to admit, spooking him a little. Why would Luke bring death to Jem? Luke really *liked* Jem . . . and quite apart from that, there wasn't a murderous bone in his body. After all he'd been through since becoming a Cola, you would think he might be quite justifiably murderous from time to time, but he was the gentlest person, outside Mia, that Gideon knew.

'Luke,' he said softly, across the back seat of the discreetly armoured people carrier they were travelling in. His brother pulled his gaze away from the view of passing trees and raised an eyebrow at him.

'Do you ever think . . . about Catherine?' he asked, his voice muffled to Jem and Annie by the sound of the engine. Luke stared back at him for a few seconds, almost vacantly, and then he signed *I try not to.*

'But . . . you must do. Sometimes. I know you must because *I* do. I can't forget her,' Gideon murmured back.

She's dead, Luke signed abruptly and turned back to the window, but Gideon couldn't give up.

'I know she's dead,' he said, as a mental image of their pretty, laughing smiling sister flickered in his mind. 'And gone—and not able to hurt us ever again. But I sometimes wonder how you feel about her. You're so . . . shut off, sometimes.'

Luke realized his brother wasn't giving up. He gave a short sigh. And then he began to sign fast, jerkily, allowing the anger of his words to judder through his hands. *She made us love-her and then she sucked all the power out of every Cola she could lay her hands on and then she dragged me to France, wrenching my speech out of me on the way, used me as a human Cola battery for months on end . . . and tried to bury me alive as a finale. How do you think I feel about her?*

'Bloody angry, I'm guessing,' muttered Gideon. '*I* am. Remember I thought you were both dead for ages.'

Why are we talking about her? Luke shrugged at him and widened his eyes behind his glasses. *We beat her. We won. It's over.*

'It's just . . . that message from Lisa. *The dark twin has death for you.* It sounded like someone was trying to mess with our minds. It made me think about her again.'

87

Luke looked at him stonily and then lifted his hands again. *Catherine is NOT getting to us from beyond the grave. Lisa would KNOW if it was her, wouldn't she? She'd know.*

Gideon nodded. 'I guess you're right. She *would* know. It's just another barmy Lisa riddle. I think she probably just misses us,' he grinned, 'and wanted an excuse to call us.' He settled back and joined Luke in watching the pretty island countryside pass by. He still felt uneasy, but there was nothing to do about it. He wasn't about to warn Jem about something so vague—especially when it sounded as if it was a warning about Luke. Which it couldn't possibly be.

Luke wasn't taking in the view of the countryside. His mind was tinged with a familiar greyness. It wasn't the horror that he minded reliving when he thought of Catherine. He could see now the small circular wooden room he had been kept in, weak and dumb, for months on end. Fed, watered, bathed, led to the toilet, led back again, pressed deep into sleep by her warm, greedy, power draining hands. It was horrific to be kept in a living coma so his parasite sister could feed on him, boosting her Cola powers at his expense.

But what horrified him more was that in spite of all she had put him through, he still felt an appalling connection with her. Their callous triplet sister had been his only link to life for so very long. He had hated her. *Hated and feared her.* But he had still . . . he had *still* loved her.

And any other girl he'd come to care about since—Mia, Lisa, Jennifer: the Cola girls—he could not completely trust. Even though his mind told him they were absolutely his friends and would do anything for him, it seemed Catherine, as well as wiping out his voice, had wiped out all hope of trusting girls again. This was something he had not told Gideon. It lay like an immovable cold pebble in his soul.

Catherine was dead. But would she ever be *gone*?

Lydia held her breath. The man had not seen her. He should have heard her, but she realized why he hadn't. He was fiddling with a small black gadget in his hands. And now he seemed to be *aiming* it at something in the bushes further up the garden. He also had some in-ear headphones on, attached to the gadget (even though it didn't look like any kind of MP3 player she'd ever seen). Otherwise she was certain he would have been alerted by the tree branches creaking. And if she moved again now, he almost certainly would hear her.

Her heart thumped so loudly in her chest she felt sure he'd hear *that* at any moment, but so far his attention was fixed on his headset and now he was turning to stare up towards the house. Who was he? What was he doing in Gideon and Luke's garden?

A sudden loud flapping and cawing from some squabbling pigeons and magpies further up the lawn gave her enough noise cover to slide back off the branch and jump down behind her own fence again. She stood, shaking, staring at the wood panelling. *What's wrong with you?* she asked herself. *Doesn't matter who's in their garden—he must be a friend or something. Just drop the money back another time.* But still she waited and then peered through a knothole in the fence, trying to locate the man. He was still there. And she knew he was not behaving like a friend who'd just dropped round. Sitting alone, hidden from the house, with a big black holdall. He must be a burglar, casing the house and planning to break in.

She should call the police. And she nearly did, reaching for the mobile in her pocket. But of course, she couldn't. Even if she didn't give her name and address they could trace the call and then come to talk to her about witness statements and all that—and they would find out about Mum.

No. She stood, anchored to the grass by indecision and nerves. Gideon and Luke had saved her life . . . and helped Matty. And given her money in a clumsy effort to help her out. She couldn't just shrug and let a burglar ransack their house. Perhaps she could frighten the burglar off. Yes! With Fish!

Quietly she turned and ran back to the house. 'Fish!' she called and the terrier ran happily out to her through the open kitchen door. '*Fish!* Look!' She held up Fish's favourite thing—a deflated plastic ball which his canines had punctured into a crescent some weeks ago, but with which he never tired of playing. She made as if to throw it and Fish ran up the small lawn, tail wagging frantically, little paws dancing about in delighted anticipation. She pretended to throw and he darted towards the fence with a yelp of delight and then turned around in confusion. No ball. He looked up at her, affronted, and began to bark. She teased him some more, making him bark more agitatedly.

And then she ran up towards him, shouting loudly: 'What? Is there someone over the fence, Fish? I didn't think anyone was in. Oh dear— what if it's a burglar? Maybe I should phone the police!'

She pressed her eye to the knot hole again, panting, her heart still making panicky rhythms. There was no man in her view now, but the bushes to the left of the garden were swinging, as if someone had recently pushed through them and fled. *Good!* She let out a shaky sigh of relief and rested her forehead against the wood.

3.5 centimetres away on the other side, the smiling man pressed the silencer attachment of his handgun directly between her eyes. He weighed up the options. A dead girl in a neighbouring garden would, of course, attract attention. But that might even be helpful for a short while. A useful distraction. Or . . . perhaps not. She wasn't going to phone anyone. He could hear the fakery in her— almost *smell* her need to hide something. Sometimes liars prosper. He tucked the weapon away and sank silently to the foot of the fence. The girl's panicky breathing slowed and she stepped away, her dog yapping for attention, and wandered back to her house, unaware of how close she had come to death. It seemed to be a day for second thoughts, reflected the smiling man as he departed, remotely switching the cameras back on with a press of his thumb when he was well out of their scope. He hoped he wasn't losing his touch.

Luke prodded Gideon sharply as their car climbed the hill towards Annie's cottage. *Look!* he signed. *It's her!*

Gideon was surprised to see Lydia leaning on their fence, with Matty and Fish scuffing about in the kerb nearby. She was smiling. A little too tightly, he thought.

'Hello, you!' he called, sliding his window down as the car pulled up.

'Hi!' she gave a little wave. As soon as they were all out, Gideon introduced her to Annie and then did the same for Matty and Fish.

'Oh! So *you're* the fossil huntress,' smiled Annie. 'I've heard all about you. We were just going to have tea and cake. Why don't you come in and join us?'

For a few seconds Lydia looked . . . almost nervous, thought Gideon. But then she smiled and said, 'Thanks—we'd love to. C'mon, Matty!' She glanced back at Annie. 'Is it OK for Fish to come in? He can go into the back garden. He won't make a mess or anything.'

'Of course, love,' said Annie. 'He can come into the house with us if you like.'

'Oh no,' said Lydia, quickly. 'The garden will be fine.' She had been working this out all the way round to the house, tugging Matty and Fish along with her. She had planned to send Fish in anyway, around the side gate—or under it if necessary (Fish was a terrier and could get through quite small gaps). She just wanted to be sure the burglar really had gone. And when the car had pulled up she'd rearranged her plan fast. After all, Gideon *had* invited her round.

They opened the gate and she sent Fish trotting happily through. 'Go find the man,' she whispered in his furry ear.

Then they went inside for tea in the warm kitchen, sitting down at the scrubbed pine table. And it seemed *everyone* was looking at her. Annie, with a warm, motherly smile as she patted Matty's head and asked if he wanted squash—and was that OK, Lydia? And Gideon and Luke, grinning with just a hint of unease which confirmed that they were indeed her anonymous cash donors. And Uncle Jem, with a cool appraisal which panicked her so much she nearly ran out. Maybe he was a policeman. He had that air about him.

'I've seen you before, haven't I?' Annie was saying. 'You take your little brother to school most days, don't you? I see you when I go to the Post Office. You're always walking very fast!'

'Because we're always late,' said Lydia, grinning ruefully across her tea cup. She eyed the golden home-made Victoria sponge, filled with a thick red layer of jam and topped with powdery drifts of icing sugar, and an odd emotion clamped her throat shut for a few seconds. Mum used to make sponge cake—exactly like this.

'I haven't seen your mum out much though,' went on Annie. 'Not for a while.'

'No, well, Mum has agoraphobia.' The words were out of her mouth before she had stopped to think. Idiot! It was the line she gave everyone— fear of open spaces—but only yesterday she'd fed Gideon and Luke the lie that Mum was up the shop. An agoraphobic, up the shop? Now she couldn't help her eyes flickering across to them. Gideon was not reacting at all and Luke just gave her the smallest smile and nod. Oh damn, damn, damn. They definitely *knew*.

'I—I'd better just check on Fish,' she muttered, and clattered out through the kitchen door at speed, coming to rest on the cool tiles of the veranda a few seconds later. What would that nice lady think of her? She was as jumpy as a squirrel. She heard Matty chatting away to Annie back in the kitchen, unconcerned. He'd better not give the game away. *Just eat your squash and cake, Matty,* she mentally urged him.

Luke and Gideon sat down on either side of her a few moments later. They said nothing for a while and then she sighed and pulled the money out of her pocket. 'I suppose this is from you,' she said.

'Money? From us? You've got to be joking,' said Gideon, without a drop of surprise.

'I came to give it back,' she said. 'I really don't need it.'

'Well, donate it to charity then,' said Gideon. 'It's not ours.'

96

She sighed again and felt like crying. It was so much *harder* when people were nice to her.

'She is coming back, you know,' she said, flipping the notes in her fingers. 'Soon. And we're fine. Just fine.'

Gideon surprised himself by putting an arm around her. 'Good,' he said. Luke put his arm across too, resting his hand on Gideon's shoulder—a Reader twin shelter. They felt her shoulders start to shake and her head dropped a little while she scrabbled in her pocket for a tissue. Nobody spoke for a minute, during which time she blew her nose and took some steadying breaths.

'You're nice people,' she said, at length, shrugging away from them.

'If . . . if she doesn't come back by, say, July,' said Gideon, 'will you get help?'

'She'll be back by then. Sooner. Maybe tomorrow.'

'Do you know where she is?' Gideon played with Fish's ears as the terrier scooted closer to his mistress, sensing her upset.

'I have an idea of it. I think she's safe—being looked after. She . . . she got very depressed after my dad died.' Lydia stared at the notes rolled up in one hand, no longer seeing the money at all. 'For the first year she was OK, but then, just when you'd think she'd be getting stronger, she got worse. First she just wouldn't get out of bed. And then she wouldn't go to sleep—she was up all night. She started getting panicky about stupid stuff—like earthquakes and volcanoes and global warming. Like, if she stayed up all night she could somehow guard us against natural disasters! I couldn't stop her worrying. No matter what I said. Anything bad on the news just tipped her over and she'd be in such a state. Sometimes she couldn't let us leave the house. I had to be tough on her when it was a school day.' She gulped and scrubbed her eyes with the damp tissue. 'I broke the TV. I pulled the wires out on the plug so it wouldn't work. So she switched to the radio. Radio Four. God, I *hate The Today Programme*. A week of that and anyone would lose the will to live. It's so *miserable*. I took out the batteries.'

Gideon continued to rub Fish's ears and he bit his lip as he imagined Lydia desperately trying to protect her mother from all the bad news the media could serve up.

'It's my fault she left,' she went on. 'I got her to start meditating. Borrowed some books and

CDs from the library and she started using them. And then she started talking about this retreat in Wales all the time—like it was the only answer. And . . . I think that's where she went. When we got back from school one day she was gone. She took clothes and stuff and she just went. She left a note saying she would be back as soon as she was strong enough. She left money for us too—enough for a week, maybe two. So . . . we waited.'

'And she didn't come back,' said Gideon. 'How long has it been now?'

'Five months,' said Lydia.

There was an appalled silence before Gideon went on, 'How are you managing?'

'Well, all the bills are paid automatically and there's plenty of money in Mum's account because of the insurance pay out when Dad died. It's just food that's the problem . . . and clothes soon. Shoes. I can't get her money out of the bank.'

'So . . . you get fossils to sell,' concluded Gideon. He felt a wave of respect for this girl. He could not imagine being able to cope so well. 'But why not ask for help?' he said, although he knew the answer.

'We have no other family,' she said. 'We'll be put into care. Split up, probably. I'm not having that.

We were fostered for two weeks after Dad died, while Mum was under sedation. I'm *never* letting that happen again.'

Luke signed at Gideon. 'Luke says *his* foster mum was brilliant,' said Gideon. 'They're not all bad.'

'She wasn't bad. She just wasn't Mum. And next time we might be split up because of our ages. Loads of people want little kids. Hardly anyone wants a teenager. She only took us both because it was short term. I'm not risking it,' she said. She stood up and turned, surveying them both with serious amber eyes.

'But—haven't you tried to find your mum?' went on Gideon, trying to get his head around the scale of Lydia's problem.

'*How?* I did call some places where I thought she might be—there's one which comes up on her bank statement each month—the retreat place in Wales. I called there a few times but I couldn't get any real information from them without telling them who I was. And if I try too hard there'll be too many questions. And then the social services will come and then . . . well, then I don't get to make any more decisions, do I?' She paused and watched Fish run off back down the garden and begin foraging happily under a bush. 'You're not going to tell anyone, are you?'

'No,' said Gideon. 'As long as you promise us something.'

'What?' She looked edgy.

'We'll swap phone numbers, and when we're gone you'll call us—at least once a week—and let us know how it's going. Or we'll call you.' Gideon didn't expect her to say yes—or to do it if she said she would—but he had to ask.

'OK,' she said. 'Deal. And . . . thank you.' She pushed the money into her shorts pocket, her cheeks reddening, then sat down once more as Fish ran up to her, and began playing with his ears again.

Gideon got out his phone. She looked up at him, alarmed.

'It's all right—I'm just phoning a mate, not the police!' said Gideon and stepped away down the garden to the small hummock next to the shed— the only spot which offered just one dodgy bar of cell coverage.

Mia picked up. 'Lisa's nails are drying,' she said, with a smile in her tone. 'She says what do you want? And did anyone die yesterday?'

'Um . . . no,' said Gideon. 'We all still seem to be alive. Sorry to disappoint her. But I need some help. Dowsing help.' Mia relayed his words and Lisa shouted out, *Fill out an SCN slip when you get back! You're on holiday!'*

'Tell her to stop being a brat and pick up,' Gideon told Mia. She giggled, passed on the message and then there was a scuffly noise as Lisa snatched up the phone.

'Better be important, Reader,' she snapped. 'This is very expensive polish and if it chips I've lost a whole nail's worth and you'll have to pay for it out of your chocolate money.'

'That's what I love about you, Lees,' said Gideon. 'All your priorities are in the right place.'

'Well?'

'I need you to dowse someone for me.' He turned his face away from Lydia's view.

'Who?'

'Um . . . her name's . . . Mrs Carr. From Bonchurch on the Isle of Wight—but she might be somewhere in Wales now.'

'Dead or alive?'

'Alive . . . I hope.'

'And . . . ?'

'Well—that's kind of it . . . '

'Gideon—do you think I'm a 118 call service? You haven't even told me her first *name*! Who is she? Why do you want her? Where's my connection?'

Gideon had to admit to himself that it was a tall order. Usually Lisa dowsed while touching something connected to the lost person. Half a name and a vague location was pushing it a bit. 'She's the mum of a girl we've made friends with— she's gone missing. I can't tell you much more than this.'

'Ooooh—a giiii-iiirl!' Lisa's voice immediately changed. 'You faa-aancy her!'

'Yes—if it helps!' snapped Gideon.

'Put her on then.'

'She's not—'

'Yes she is. She's within ten feet of you—I can sense it right through you. Put her on.'

'She won't understand.'

'Doesn't matter.'

Gideon waved at Lydia, sitting companionably with Luke and Fish, and urged her across to him. She came, looking ill at ease as she saw he was still on the phone. 'Can't move—dodgy signal,' he explained as she drew closer. 'My friend Lisa just wanted to ask you something about fossils.' He pushed the phone into her palm and she put it to her ear, looking wary.

Gideon had not tried to fill Lisa in further; he knew it wasn't necessary. He could hear her talking as she effortlessly slid into Lydia's mind. 'Hi, Lydia—I'm Lisa. Gid says you're into all this fossil stuff, yeah?'

'Um . . . yes,' said Lydia.

'So are ammonites the little curly ones or the cave thingies inside stones with, like, crystals?'

Lydia raised her eyebrows. Gideon's friend sounded extraordinarily dim. 'OK—ammonites are fossilized remains of sea creatures and yes, they curl around, like the inside of a snail's shell. And the little crystal caves inside stones are geodes.'

'Brilliant! That's what I thought. Thanks. Hand me back to Gideon now.'

Baffled, Lydia passed back the phone before shrugging at Gideon and making her way back to Luke.

'Got anything?' muttered Gideon.

'Hmmm,' said Lisa. 'I'll let you know.'

'Don't just forget!' warned Gideon. 'It's important.'

'I know,' said Lisa. 'I've just been in her head. I will try, OK?'

'Thanks,' said Gideon and ended the call.

'Come on, you lot,' Annie called out of the kitchen window. 'Tea's getting cold.'

8

Luke dreamed of Catherine that night. It was Gideon bringing it up in the car, he guessed. In his dream Catherine was just about to say sorry. Just about to explain that she had never meant to hurt him—not really. That she had been possessed or something—unable to control what was happening. She was also just about to touch his head and give him back his speech.

And then he was lying helpless in the ground, slowly being buried in earth, unable to escape. His face was the last thing that would be covered, even though his eyes were wide open, pleading, and Catherine, her shiny dark hair in a plait and her green eyes sparkling with fun, could clearly see he was alive. *'You're all flat!'* she said to him, cheerily, resting her arm on the shovel. *'I've used up all your*

Cola power and there's none left!' She pouted and shrugged. *'Byeee.'* And then she took up the shovel and the cold earth hit his face as she sang out, *'Attention au jumeau foncé, Luc! Est-ce toi? Est-ce toi?'* And then he was suddenly awake, gasping, sweaty and agitated, his sheet knotted around his feet and his mouth dry, staring into the dark.

He sat up in bed and reached for his glass of water, careful to be quiet and not wake Gideon— although Gideon could usually sleep through pretty much anything. The cup knocked his watch off the table and he instinctively caught it with his mind, freezing it in mid air, lifting it and then lowering it silently back onto his bedside table. Not for the first time he wondered about the recurring dream. The dream was true to real life only in one way: it never ended properly. In reality he had been saved by Gideon, Owen and Tyrone, and Mia, well before he had been buried in the French woodland. And in reality Catherine had never attempted to explain or excuse her behaviour. He knew his situation with his dead sister would never end properly, either. She was long gone. She had exploded in a ball of flame over the North Sea more than a year ago. She

hadn't been in human form, he'd later learned—
she'd been a huge black raven or something,
having finally managed, in the last half hour of
her life, to steal Dax Jones's shapeshifting power.
It was the only power she had not already stolen
and it turned out to be her last.

But now he wrinkled his forehead. Something
about the dream *was* different. This time she had
said something to him . . . something about the
dark twin. In French, she'd been singing, *'Look out
for the dark twin, Luke! Is it you? Is it you?'* Obviously
that was Gideon's doing too, with his message
from Lisa about the 'dark twin bringing death'
or something. What else had Catherine said in
his dream? She'd still been talking as the earth
covered his mouth and nose. He closed his eyes;
tried to recapture the wash of sleep which still
held his subconscious cinema. *Who will bring death,
then, Luke?* she had asked as she hefted another
shovelful of earth at him. *Which twin? It will be ONE
of you . . .* Only that made no sense because he was
the only dark twin.

He knew that it was twaddle, as Annie would have
put it. Twaddle and tosh. In the morning he would
laugh about it. But right now he couldn't, so he got

out of bed, went to the toilet, came back, treading quietly across the room past Gideon's gently snoring form, and paused to look out of the window. A dim light showed in the upstairs window of a house diagonally opposite. That would be Clara or . . . who was the new guy? John? The other special operative, anyway. Hard-faced man with thin lips. Well, they couldn't *all* look like James Bond, he guessed. One of them was awake, reporting in to Control every half hour with the all-clear on the security cameras. What a dull job. He yawned, reminding himself not to become a special operative for the Government and almost immediately remembering that this was certainly what he *would* become. With his Cola power he was far too useful to end up being a teacher or a writer, both of which he would have pursued if his life had been different.

He saw Clara's outline in the window and waved goodnight to her. She didn't wave back. She wouldn't have even if she'd seen him. She took her work very seriously and would give her life for it, he wouldn't mind betting. He should remember this, when he was having his 'girl trust issues'. He shook his head at his dim reflection in the glass. Having some girl who claimed to love you attempt to bury you alive was *some* excuse. *Remember*, Clara was a girl. She didn't love him and she would still give her life for him and Gideon. Although it *was* her job. Still . . . Clara would.

A few hours later, Clara would.

'The Devil's Chimney!' said Gideon at breakfast the next morning. 'Come *on*! I want to see it!'

'It's just another landslip,' said Jem. 'Haven't you had enough of those for one week?'

'No—it's not a beach, it's all green and woodsy and atmospheric and it's got this narrow little steep passage which goes down, down into the rock,' breathed Gideon with drama, peering at the *Places To See On The Island* booklet he'd picked up at Brading. 'It's cool. Me and Luke can time each other to run up and down the chimney. I'm trying to get him fit, don't you know?'

Luke raised an unimpressed eyebrow as he buttered his toast. It was true he was less energetic than his brother but only because he loved to spend hours reading rather than haring about like a daddy-long-legs on a sugar rush.

'We could walk it—it's really close,' went on

Gideon but Jem shook his head. He didn't want them walking too far away from the armoured cars.

'Not sure about the weather,' said Jem. 'Forecast is for rain—maybe even thunder.'

'Not till this afternoon,' said Gideon. 'We can do the Devil's Chimney this morning and come back here for the afternoon. Maybe . . . maybe have Lydia and Matty round again after they get back from school.'

'That would be nice,' smiled Annie, pouring more tea into Jem's cup. 'You like her, don't you, Gideon?'

Gideon ducked his head over his bowl of Shreddies to hide his blush. 'Yeah—and Matty,' he mumbled. 'They're great.'

Annie smiled a knowing smile and Luke laughed in his soft raspy way. 'She's awfully . . . grown up . . . for a teenager,' went on Annie. 'Really takes care of little Matty. Because their mum's unwell, I suppose. It's hard on children when they have to be carers. And after losing their dad too. I wish I could do more to help. I could call in and see their mum and offer to have them round from time to time.'

'No—don't do that!' The words were out past

the munched up Shreddies and milk and in the air before Gideon could stop himself. 'She . . . she's quite proud,' he tried to explain. 'Doesn't accept charity or anything. Better just to tell Lydia so she and Matty can come round when they want to.'

'Well, maybe,' said Annie. 'But I want to be sure their mum knows where they are.'

'It's pretty late already . . . I can't believe how long you two sleep for,' said Jem, checking his watch. 'We'd better get going soon, if you're really set on the Devil's Chimney. Don't want to end up getting washed into the sea by that storm.'

'Day trip time,' Clara called down the stairs to John. Jem had just been in touch on the secure line and informed her of Gideon and Luke's itinerary for the day. She grinned. She quite fancied the Devil's Chimney. She'd been there years ago when she was a kid and liked its spooky quiet atmosphere—the way it felt as if it might just sigh, give up and slide away into the sea at any time. She got into jeans, a sweatshirt, and her craggy-soled walking boots, then added a many-pocketed sleeveless vest which held the gadgetry which enabled her to keep in close communication with Jem, John, and Control. It also hid her handgun, holstered high under her left arm. It was reassuring to have it back in place after the beach visits where she needed to keep such hardware in a bag.

John got into the Jeep ahead of her and started the engine as she locked up the cottage. The tinted glass reflected a sunny day in a quiet island lane. She would have liked to get those windows open and keep the fresh air flowing on their journey, so that she could enjoy the heady scent of early summer blossom on the breeze, but John insisted on air con and sealed glass. It was more secure and she would never argue with that. She was clearly spending far too much time thinking about summer holidays as a kid. She smiled at her self-indulgence and opened the passenger door, noticing Jem and the boys heading out in their grey VW people carrier across the road.

'OK. Day four in the Big Brother Jeep,' she quipped, with a bad Geordie accent, as she pulled the door shut. 'What's with the plastic?' A thin sheet of plastic had been pulled across the dashboard.

'In case it gets messy,' said John. 'Clara—I'd like you to meet Yanos.'

Shocked, Clara spun in her seat and saw a dark-haired man sitting in the rear of the Jeep. He was smiling and she noticed a white flash through his hair at one temple.

'What the hell—?'

'Calm down—he's been sent,' said John, reaching for the car stereo.

Clara eyed the man, who was still smiling. Plastic crackled under her walking boots. The foot-well was lined with it too. The hair prickled up across her arms. John turned the radio on and a heavy bass line pounded out of it at high volume.

Clara swallowed, keeping calm. 'What has he been sent for?'

The man smiled even more, lifted one eyebrow in a roguish way and brought out a .22 calibre pistol, partially wrapped in a plastic bag. 'To kill you.'

She went for the Glock but there was no time.

He shot her in the centre of her forehead. The radio hid the thud. The plastic caught the mess.

The slope down to the Devil's Chimney was deceptively gentle; a lawn of patchy grass dotted with trees and shrubs. From the small roadside car park a rough path wound across the lawn at an angle, leading them past a cottage-style tea room—the Smuggler's Haven—to their right and on towards some thick green undergrowth through which distant blue glimpses of the sea could be caught. There were very few people about—just an elderly couple making their way across to the tea room.

A sign warned off the disabled as the path dropped a steep couple of steps and offered a route north or south along the ivy-bound cliff. 'This way!' called Gideon, heading south after consulting more detail on the sign. In seconds they were walking along the first gentle slope; a narrow path against the cliff face, craggy rock and clinging vegetation to their right. To their left a low rock wall prevented them from tumbling into a wide tree-filled chasm below. Birds twittered and chiff-chaffed endlessly and flitted amid branches which twisted and tangled in all directions. Trees that had begun their lifespan reaching for the sun had been, at some stage, abruptly tipped by landslip and forced to angle their growth as best they could from wherever they had come to rest. It was a collapsed woodland—a huge game of jack straws for ever sprawling towards the sea.

'Weird,' said Gideon, noticing an elderly iron-and-wood slat bench which dangled almost vertically from the edge of a rocky outcrop three or four metres below the path. The path it had once rested on had long since fallen away.

They came to the Devil's Chimney with whoops of excitement from Gideon. Here some authority had set tubular iron banisters in place to guide visitors down steep concrete steps into the thin sleeve of space between two looming planes of rock. Gnarled roots from the more successful trees clenched the topsoil at the entrance to this damp stone well, and fans of fern decorated the rough walls as Gideon and Luke descended into the cool with Jem close behind. Only a thin blade of sunlight wobbled across one wall, narrowing to a sliver as they moved down.

Gideon inhaled the mineral scent of ancient earth, dust, lichen, and moss and ran both his palms across the stone on either side, which pressed in ever tighter the further down he stepped. He raised his eyes and immediately understood the name of the place—it was just like looking up an old stone chimney; the bright summer sun glinting down from many metres above, broken up by roots and trunks and waving leaves. A few creepers had attempted to get down here, dangling their pale fibrous ropes across the greys and greens and coppery browns of the rock face. But at the very foot of the chimney nothing grew. The birdsong was muted down here and the air was very still.

'Wouldn't do for the obese,' muttered Jem, pulling his elbows in. In places it was very narrow. 'Well—that's it. Devil's Chimney. Happy now?' It had taken only a minute to descend, turn a right-angled corner and arrive on the next plateau of landslip.

'No! Again! Again!' shouted Gideon and turned round to run back in.

Jem sighed and pressed in his earpiece. 'You up there, Clara? John?' he checked. He'd seen the Jeep pull in before they left the roadside car park and John Farrier had signalled in his earpiece that they would be a minute behind.

'Yup,' came back a voice. It was John, a little crackly. The deep broken ravines did not help the signal. 'We're good. Clara says you were right about the walking boots.'

Jem smiled. He'd reminded Clara about the

Island and its hills, telling her in no uncertain terms to pack walking boots along with flip-flops. 'All clear up there?' he checked.

'Affirmative,' came back John. 'Deserted. We're at the top of the chimney. Shall we come down? You all going on further?'

'Come on—time me!' Gideon was saying, checking his watch alongside Luke. 'See how long it takes me to make it to the top and back down again. And then I'll time *you*.' Luke was grinning and shaking his head. 'Come on! It'll do you good, you weed!' chided his brother. 'Build up a bit of muscle on those spindly legs.'

Jem pushed in behind them at the bottom-most angle of the chimney—the grate—and squinted up the steep dark stairwell, but was too far back to make out the top of the steps. He didn't like this restricted view. He wanted to get the boys back up top . . . but he was treading a fine line here. If he had followed the rules to the letter they would not be here. In fact they would never have come to this island at all. It posed risks and it wasn't necessary. But the Cola Project had agreed its assets must have some holiday time and this . . . this was it. What was the point if he stopped their fun?

'Are we coming down?' prompted John.

'Negative. Wait up there for a bit,' Jem replied. 'We've got an endurance climb going on in the chimney for the next five minutes.' There was a crackle of acknowledgement deep in his ear which made him wince. Sometimes he really missed the old hand-held two way radios, clunky and visible as they were.

'Three—two—one—GO!' Gideon yelled at himself before lurching up the steps. His footfalls echoed, rebounding in dull smacks on the oppressive rock walls on either side. In a few seconds his gasps and groans could also be heard as he battled against gravity and musty air on the steep climb. 'TOP!' he yelled back down to them thirty-six seconds later, just out of view, and then 'Coming back! Keep timing!' Running down wasn't much easier. His legs were trembling from the exertion of the climb and he had to cling carefully to the iron banisters as he went or risk going head over heels. It took him almost as long to reach Luke.

Click. Luke held up his watch, revealing the seconds elapsed. Gideon slumped onto the bottom step, exhausted, and squinted at it balefully. 'I've *got* to get fitter,' he mumbled. Ten seconds later he stood up and checked his own watch. 'OK—your turn,' he told Luke. 'Three—two—one—GO!'

Luke hared away up the stairs, his hard exhalations funnelling back down to them just a few seconds into the climb. 'You should go next, Jem,' said Gideon, still catching his own lungfuls. 'You should do it in twenty seconds flat with all your SAS training.'

'Maybe another day,' said Jem. Luke's footfalls were more distant now. He must be nearing the top. They waited for his return, knowing that no shout would come from him. After forty-five seconds there was nothing.

'He's wimped out!' cackled Gideon. 'He's slumped over the top banister watching all the squiggly lines in his eyeballs. Luke! Get a move on, you wuss!'

There was no reluctant stomping back down. Jem tilted his head and listened hard for breathing and then pushed past Gideon and began to climb the steps.

'He's coming,' said Gideon. 'He's just a slowcoach.'

But Jem was running now, sprinting up the

steps at admirable speed and for the first time Gideon felt a cold tickle inside his belly. 'Jem? Can you see him?' He began to run after Jem, panic suddenly lending extra energy to his legs. 'Jem! Is he there?'

At the top of the Devil's Chimney Jem stood alone, his nostrils flared, talking to Control and turning 360 degrees, his eagle eyes reading every track. Gideon saw the look on his face and felt his insides slip like the land. He heard three mundane words which filled him with horror.

'Repeat: asset lost.'

9

Lydia took Matty to school and then went home to get a bit of housework done before heading back to the fossils. It was a rare occasion when she didn't have to fake a sick note email from her 'housebound' mother to have some time off to go fossil hunting while Matty was being looked after at infants. Today was a teacher training day at her school, but not at Matty's. As she cleaned the bathroom she decided she would just take Fish for a quick run in the woodland that backed on to Bonchurch Chute . . . and then she'd go back to the beach. She'd decided to splash out a bit on the bus back to the cliff fall and didn't want to risk a dog wee problem mid journey.

Yes, she *could* afford maybe to take it easy for a few days—she had £200 plus the £40 left from her last fossil money—but she knew that other fossil hunters would be swarming the newborn cliff face by now and she couldn't bear to think that all the pickings would be gone before she returned. And, as ever, she had to prepare for the fact that Mum *wouldn't* be back in a couple of weeks. In her mind she often saw herself walking along a high thin ridge, usually leading Matty by the hand. Mostly she glanced down the green sunny slope to her right, the view which reassured her 'All will be well; keep going, she'll be back any day.' But she was not blind to the darker slope to her left; the one which plummeted to a barren grey valley; which warned, 'She may never come back. Be prepared.' To keep her balance she had to be aware of both sides.

'Come on, Fish,' she called, late that morning, attaching the lead to the little dog's worn leather collar, barely visible amid his tufty black coat. He gave several small wuffs and his claws snickered across the tiles on the front porch as he danced with excitement.

Lydia locked the house carefully behind her, slung her fossil satchel over her shoulder with a practised shrug, and pulled a wide-brimmed cotton hat across her coppery hair, which she'd tugged into two thick plaits. It was sunny today and on the beach it would be hot work. She had even smoothed a little Factor 20 across her bare legs and arms, still hearing her mother's sunburn warnings in her head. Her shorts and T-shirt, at least, still fitted OK. But she sighed as she realized that reaching up with the hat had exposed a lot of skinny midriff which she might also have to cover with lotion. She would have to buy a couple of cheap tops from Tesco soon. Her walking boots, too, were rubbing just a little on her toes, and this worried her most because she couldn't hope to replace *them* for less than £40. And when you were working the cliff face you *had* to have proper boots. A falling rock could break your toes and a trip to casualty was the last thing she and Matty needed.

'OK,' she said, aloud. 'The sun is shining. I have a day off school and money for the bus and lots of fabulous fossils to find—but first, a walk in the woods.' She made herself smile away the worries and it helped. By the time she'd turned into the next road up she was feeling surprisingly chirpy. As she approached Luke and Gideon's place she knew they were part of the reason why. It had been unexpectedly comforting to talk to them yesterday;

to feel their concern but not have to fear their actions. She clicked her tongue, though, when she realized that she had failed to tell them about the burglar. She should have done that . . . especially once they knew her secret and she could be sure the police would not backtrack to her; they would have protected her, she was certain.

But he had gone anyway—fled when Fish did his big bark thing—and there'd been no sign of him later either. They had scared him off and he probably wouldn't be back. Just a passing opportunist.

'Hello, Lydia!'

She jolted, shocked from her thoughts. It was Annie, standing at her gate. 'No school today?' she asked.

'Hi, Annie,' smiled Lydia. 'No—teacher training day. So I get to walk Fish!'

'Where are you off to? The woods?'

'Yes,' said Lydia. 'Give him a bit of a run around. Then we're going to the beach.'

'More fossil hunting?' Annie eyed her satchel with amusement.

'Maybe,' she shrugged. 'It's a bit of a hobby.'

'Good for you,' said Annie, stepping out of the gate and closing it behind her. 'Can I walk some of the way with you? I need to stretch my legs.'

Lydia held down a flicker of panic. She *liked* Annie. The company would be nice. She just hoped her questions wouldn't get tricky. 'Yes, of course. That'll be great.'

'I need to exercise regularly,' explained Annie, falling into step with her. 'I have osteoarthritis in my hips. I've had most of both of them replaced, in fact. I won't be doing the trapeze again,' she sighed comically, 'but I *will* walk for many years to come— as long as I *do* walk. I used to go out every day with Maureen, my old friend who lived with me for a couple of years after Luke went . . . to the college. But she's gone to New Zealand now, to live near her daughter. I miss the company.'

'Well, it's nice for me to have company too,' said Lydia.

'No friends your own age living nearby?' asked Annie.

'No—they're all in Ventnor,' she said. It was true, really. She didn't add that she'd had to stop asking them back to her place, in case they worked out her situation. She'd now lost most of her friends by just cutting them off.

'Well, if you ever want a chat with another girl

about forty years older than you, you just drop in. Any time,' said Annie as they reached the trees.

They ambled along the path and Fish, let off the lead, darted ahead, zigzagging merrily from tree to tree and disappearing for minutes on end as he foraged for mystery things in the undergrowth. Lydia didn't fear for the Island's celebrated red squirrels. He was way too noisy to ever catch anything more than an old ball.

'You must miss Luke and Gideon, when they're gone,' remarked Lydia.

'I do,' said Annie. 'Luke mostly, of course, as he's been with me most of his life—but I've grown to love Gideon too. They're both . . . incredibly special. I go up to stay at their college too, three or four times a year. It's a beautiful place in the Lake District.'

Fish began to yap excitedly in the distance. He must have found another old ball, thought Lydia.

'It's tough to struggle on without the people you love,' went on Annie.

'I know,' said Lydia, before she could stop herself.

'But friends, neighbours . . . they all make up for it. Do come and see me, Lydia. I know it must be really hard for you. I suspect you've had to be a bit of a mum to Matty, haven't you?'

Lydia's heart jolted again, but Annie continued: 'Having to look after your mother and cope with losing your dad. It must knock you for six and I think maybe you don't get quite enough fun right now.'

'I—well . . . maybe,' gulped Lydia.

'So . . . seriously, sweetheart. Any time I can help, come and see me. And any time you'd like me to look after Matty so your mum can get some rest and you can go off and just be a teenager for a while . . . '

Lydia struggled, for the second time in two days, not to burst into tears. 'That's really kind . . . ' she began, but then Fish's barking rose to a whole new pitch and she was distracted. 'Um . . . I think I need to go after Fish. He sounds . . . ' She hurried down the path and peered over the edge of a drop into a mini ravine choked with straggly bushes and tangled brambles.

'Fish! Fish! What is it?' she called. Fish came running immediately. He was excited—but not happy. His tail was stiff and low and his fur was ruffled, standing on end.

'Has he found something?' called Annie, from the path a few steps above.

'Yes,' called back Lydia. 'Go on, Fish. Show me!'

As she scrambled down the steep, prickly incline, snatching handholds amid the thin branches, she felt a sudden sense of foreboding. It was gloomy down here with not much sun filtering through the leaves. She could see Fish now standing still, glancing down at something on the damp leaf litter and then back at her, with a little flash of white in his eyes and a whine in his throat. His fur was standing on end; he looked like a bottle brush. She stood straight as the ground levelled out into a narrow gulley and walked the six or seven steps towards her dog with a strange out-of-body feeling. Something pale curled through a thin patch of brambles. It made her think of a small fossil. Still. Dusty. Curled up in death. But this find was not millions of years old.

It was a hand. And without looking any further, Lydia knew it was a dead hand.

She stifled a shocked whimper, but Annie, also clambering stiffly down now, heard her. 'Lydia? What's wrong?'

She knew she had to look. She leaned closer, her hands across her mouth, and saw the arm and the shoulder. The twisted neck and dark hair caked with mud and some other matter that she just couldn't process. She shrieked when a warm hand rested on her shoulder.

'Oh hell,' sighed Annie. 'It's always dog walkers that find them, isn't it?'

The body lay bent around the trunk of a woody rhododendron, quite still inside its cave of waxy green leaves. A woman—probably in her twenties, thought Lydia, but it was hard to tell. The body already looking bleached and inanimate like a piece of woodland floor. 'I think . . . I think she's been shot. In the head,' she gulped, her breakfast rising in her throat.

Annie did not let go of her. 'I know,' she said, very calmly. 'Do you need to be sick, sweetheart?'

Lydia did not need further telling. She staggered sideways, knelt down and threw up violently, while poor Fish whined and shook at her feet.

As she gradually regained control of the spasms in her throat, Lydia heard Annie take a sharp breath and gasp out, 'No! Oh *no* . . . It's Clara!'

'You know her?' sniffed Lydia, holding on to Fish and trying to get back some sense of balance.

'Oh no,' moaned Annie, again, wrestling with her mobile phone. 'I—I can't get a signal! I've got to call Control!' She sounded full of dread—a world away from her calm reassurance a minute past.

'Control? Dial 999! Get the police!' squeaked Lydia.

'No—you don't understand. Clara *was* police—of a sort,' said Annie. 'She was detailed to protect Luke and Gideon. Oh *no*!'

'What?' Lydia blinked.

'Clara—and the new man . . . John . . . and Jem. They're special operatives, looking after the boys. And if Clara is down, the others might be too . . . and Luke and Gideon . . . oh *no*!'

'Why on earth would they need police protection?' asked Lydia.

'Help me up the bank!' Annie commanded. 'I need to get a signal *fast*.'

'What have they seen? Are they witnesses to a murder or something?' Lydia's shocked brain was working overtime as she took Annie's arm and half shoved her back up the bank, Fish almost tripping them as he stayed close for reassurance.

'No—they're Colas,' muttered Annie. 'They're . . . talented.'

'Talented—how?'

'It doesn't matter. It's just that the whole world wants them for their talent. They have to be guarded. And now . . . maybe they're not being. I don't know! I just have to reach Control!'

'But . . . what kind of talent? Are they martial arts masters or something?' It sounded ridiculous but it was all Lydia could come up with as they reached the path and Annie began walking fast along it, holding her phone up, desperate for a signal.

'No—they're . . . look—they're telekinetics!' muttered Annie. 'And you DON'T KNOW that! OK?'

Lydia dropped behind a little way and picked up Fish, wondering if Annie had just come unhinged. Seeing a dead body might have done that to her. Telekinetic meant being able to move things around with your mind, she knew that. But . . . come *on*! And then her memory banks abruptly shuffled and threw up a flashback. She was on the beach, pinned to the shingle by Gideon—and Gideon was calling to Luke, 'It's OK—you can let it go now!' And then the cliff fell.

'It's OK—you can let it go now!'

Let *what* go? The cliff? The *cliff*? Had Luke been holding back the cliff? Telekinetically?

She ran after Annie who was out of the woodland

by now and marching back along the road, still holding her phone aloft and begging the satellite gods for just one bar of a signal. There was none. The Island's cliffside villages were always a nightmare for mobiles.

'The landline!' she said, beginning to run as Lydia reached her. 'The house!'

Osteoarthritis or not, Annie ran fast, and they were back in her cottage a minute later. But as soon as she lifted the handset she gave another shout of dismay, clicking the cradle again and again. 'Nothing!' She stared at Lydia, wild-eyed, for a moment, before running into another room; a bedroom. In it was a dizzying array of tech, most of it scattered across the dressing table, including two laptops. Annie nudged them out of screensaver sleep but the screens were just blue, with >C: blinking on them.

'It's all been *cut*. We're cut off,' whispered Annie. 'How can that *be*?'

'A power cut?' offered Lydia.

'It has a back up generator! It should *never* go off!' murmured Annie. She stood, staring at nothing, for ten seconds, while Lydia just gaped and tried to follow what was going on here. 'The

Devil's Chimney!' said Annie. 'That's where they've gone. We have to go after them—warn them!' She ran back out into the hallway and swiped some car keys from the telephone table. 'I'm going to need you, Lydia!' she said. 'Can you help me? Can you run down the Devil's Chimney for me? I can't do that.'

'Yes—yes, of course!' Lydia swept Fish up into her arms again and followed Annie out onto the sunny driveway and into her Nissan Micra.

'Right,' gulped Annie, passing her the mobile. 'You keep hitting the redial button to Control and as soon as you're through, get the speaker phone on.' She pulled out of the driveway with a shriek of tyres and a fountain of gravel. 'And tell them it's a Code 47.'

10

Luke opened his eyes in the dark. His glasses were gone. He was lying on his side, his cheek pressed to a hard gritty surface, and something was tickling his face. He went to swipe it away but realized that his hands were tied behind his back. His mind swept the tickling thing away for him, whacking the curious spider through the still air in an instant. His neck hurt—more when he swallowed—and at this point he remembered what had happened.

He had reached the top of the Devil's Chimney and paused to catch one breath and check his watch before turning and haring back down the steps—and then he'd seen the new Control minder further up the path—John, his name was— signalling to him urgently. *Come up! NOW!* Luke had glanced over his shoulder, puzzled—there was no instruction being shouted up from Jem below. He walked a few steps up the sloping path towards the minder and raised two questioning palms— and that was when he was seized from behind around the neck and shoulders. A hard hand pressed into the side of his throat. The last thing he remembered was thinking this was his death.

But apparently not. Unless this was the afterlife and he very much doubted that. His eyes were working better now and he realized that he was lying at a slant under a very low ceiling of rock. He felt rock beneath him, too, and loose grit and dirt. It was some kind of cave or maybe just a skinny chasm; a gap between fallen rocks. Light was coming in, but from some distance above him. He squinted up and worked out that he must be some way down—maybe five or six metres. Too far down for much vegetation to thrive, although there was plenty of ivy and bramble across the blade of light above him. Why was he here? Had his killer dumped the body, not realizing it wasn't quite dead? He shuddered as the memory of his 'death' came back to him. No. The attack was very, very efficient—the blocking of one carotid artery. Luke had read quite a few spy thrillers and he now knew that he'd been in a 'carotid hold'—something which disabled the victim in seconds but did not kill. He didn't believe a mistake had been made. After all, why bind the wrists of a corpse? He'd been dumped here alive. Which either meant his attacker was coming back or . . . or that he or she intended to leave him to die underground in his own time. This seemed horribly familiar.

Stop stressing about why and get this rope off! his survival instinct butted in. *You've got to get out of here!* He took a long breath of air saturated with old minerals and the tang of bat urine and winced as a bolt of pain shot up through his left leg. It had been hurting all along, he now realized, but he'd pushed it to the back of his mind while he was caught up with more immediate problems. He lay still, dreading what might happen with that leg when moved. He took a deep breath and instead concentrated on the rope tightly binding his wrists behind him. It was thin but very strong: made of hemp, not nylon, his senses informed him. It was knotted expertly, several times over. Luke closed his eyes and focused on the outermost knot, teasing it apart with his mind. It was not easy. Moving things was one thing—and Luke could move mountains (literally) if he chose, albeit in chunks. But unknotting something, especially when he was so tired and fearful and in pain, was much harder. He *could* just force it off his wrists with brute tele strength—but that might take his thumb joint with it. No—he had to unwind it steadily, as if it was a bad-tempered snake. Then he would crawl out of here and find Gideon and Jem.

If my attacker hasn't found them already. He gulped, pausing on knot number two. *No. Jem is the BEST. He'll never let Gideon get hurt.*

Didn't do so well for you, though, did he? The voice sounded like Catherine—teasing and full of malicious fun. *At the very least you've got a broken leg.*

Luke closed his eyes again and focused a thin beam of telekinetic attention purely on the knots. One thing at a time.

'Damn it!' Jem pulled off his peaked cap and peered at the sleek gadgetry hidden in its lining. He did some rudimentary tweaks to the almost invisible, thread-like wires but there was no indication that they were faulty. In his heart he knew that his communications had been shut off deliberately.

Where were Clara and John Farrier? And who *was* John Farrier, for that matter? Suddenly, Jem realized he should never have allowed a replacement to come in that he didn't know, no matter how thoroughly Control vouched for him.

'Anything?' he said to Gideon as the boy peered over the low wall into the gully. Gideon looked white as he shook his head. He'd wanted to run off alone while Jem worked his way along a different path, but Jem had not let him leave his side. They had threaded back and forth along the cliff paths for the past five minutes, sometimes shouting for Luke but having no hope of hearing him shout back. He might have been able to bash a stick against something, though, if he'd fallen and been hurt. If he *hadn't* been seized by somebody. But both Jem and Gideon knew he had been. It was all too quick and too silent for anything else.

Jem grabbed Gideon's arm and they sprinted up the path to the sloping green lawn which led to the tea room and the small roadside car park. No sign of Clara and John's Jeep. And nobody in the tea room knew anything or had seen or heard anything. By the time they reached the people carrier Gideon was sweating and shaking and ready to be sick. The last time he'd lost Luke he hadn't got him back for months and months . . . and then his twin was hurt, left scarred for ever. This could *not* be happening again.

Jem was keying in to the communications system in the Jeep and then swearing and thumping the dashboard. 'It's been sabotaged,' he muttered. 'Give me yours!'

Gideon handed over his phone. He'd already tried texting Luke on it, but there had been no signal and nothing could be sent.

Jem swore again. 'No signal! Or something's jamming it. We need to get to a landline.' He leapt back out of the Jeep and seconds later he and Gideon were back in the tea rooms. The owners didn't look pleased to see him back again after his curt interrogation about his lost nephew only minutes before. 'Phone!' he demanded. 'I need to use your landline. It's an emergency.'

'Well you could,' came the reply, 'if it was working. It's been off for the past half an hour.' The woman rattled the cradle and held the receiver up to her ear. 'Dead,' she shrugged. 'I'll have to get on to BT.' But the man and the boy were already gone.

'A phone box?' Gideon stared at Jem as he scrambled into the car. All the state of the art equipment the government could supply—no good! And now Luke's fate rested on finding a working phone box?

'Yes,' said Jem, through gritted teeth. 'Buckle up. I think there's one further along this road. If the gods are smiling it'll be in working order. Or we'll go to a house. We've got to reach Control.'

'Won't they be on alert anyway, if you don't report in?' said Gideon, pulling the seat belt across with shaking hands.

'In theory—but if John or Clara checks in on my behalf they may not.'

'But why would they do that? They've been attacked too, haven't they? Their Jeep's vanished. They must have been hijacked.'

'Maybe,' said Jem.

Gideon's jaw dropped as he took in the enormity of Jem's single word response. Jem thought this was an inside job. That John and Clara—or at least one of them—were their enemies.

'Oh *no*,' he groaned as Jem pulled out onto the road. They sped off, breaking the speed limit, and hurtled along the narrow winding lane towards the nearest village with its landline phone box. But after just twenty seconds of high speed twisting and turning which had Gideon clinging to the leather strap above the passenger door, Jem gave a sharp cry of fury. 'DAMN!' and there were two loud bangs and the car began to weave about.

'STINGER!' yelled Jem. 'Gideon—get DOWN!' The car bucked and slewed on the steeply cambered road surface, veering across the oncoming lane towards a steep unguarded drop filled with dark vegetation. A flapping, thudding noise beneath them told Gideon all the tyres were blown out. They'd driven over some kind of tyre wrecking trap.

'HOLD ON!' bawled Jem as the car crunched across the edge of the road and spun 180 degrees in the air, teetering by the axis of its undercarriage on the edge of the tarmac for a few seconds before it plunged down into the drop. The cracking and tearing noise was incredible as they hit the thin branches of slender trees and tangled shrubs. Gideon thought they might go right over in a somersault, but the people carrier ended up on its side, sliding a few feet down as the vegetation gave up the fight. Leaves and twigs and pale branches abruptly pressed up against Jem's closed window like a hastily painted abstract of woodland art. More of them scraped and knocked across the undercarriage while the contents of the car—spare trainers, a tin of travel sweets, sunglasses, two half empty bottles of water, the small change in the arm rest and a bottle of Factor 15 sun lotion—rained through the air and struck the inside windows on the driver's side with cracks and chinks.

There wasn't a single second to draw breath. Jem was unbuckling Gideon's belt, yelling 'OUT! OUT!' even as his charge slumped sideways and nearly fell onto him. A second later Gideon was scrambling up again, trying to get the door open. It was too heavy at this angle and now he pressed the button to open the window and it began to whirr down, allowing bruised leaves and twigs to drop in on top of them. 'COME ON, GIDEON! OUT!' bellowed Jem. 'They're coming!' And his gun was already in his hand, trained ahead past Gideon's shoulder. Trembling, Gideon began to heave himself up through the open window.

'NO—back! Get in the BACK!' Jem suddenly yelled, abruptly changing the plan and grabbing him back in by one shoulder. And Gideon saw why. Two men had emerged at the edge of the road, peering down at them. One was John, the replacement minder, holding a heavy mesh of spiked metal over one arm. The *stinger* which he had obviously just thrown across the road to trap them. The other was a dark-haired man who was smiling.

'The first one to move a muscle is a dead man!' shouted Jem. His hand on the gun was as steady as stone, although the veins on his forehead bulged.

'Well then, I won't move,' smiled the dark-haired man. 'Although I cannot speak for my friend here.'

John gave the dark-haired man an uneasy glance and then peered down at Jem. 'Just do as he says,' he said to Jem in a flat voice. 'You're not going anywhere and you know it. We've got the other boy.'

'I can take you out right now,' warned Jem.

And so could I, thought Gideon. *You traitor.* The fury rising up in him was so intense there might be no stopping it anyway. With a sudden jolt of white heat searing through his solar plexus, Gideon took control of the stinger. The belt of spiked metal, designed to be thrown fluidly into the path of an oncoming vehicle and wreck its tyres and wheels, was as easy to move as paper in his fingers.

There was a yelp of shock from John as the

144

stinger suddenly writhed up off his arm like an angry cobra.

'GIDEON!' yelled Jem, with warning in his voice, but Gideon did not stop. He sent the stinger's tail into a vicious swipe across John's face. The man twisted within the lethally sharp ribbon of spikes and roared as his face was lacerated. He struggled to escape the tightening coils which were now enveloping his shoulders and torso, and as he vainly tried to shake free a shower of blood spattered like red pennies across the rear passenger window.

It should have worked. It should have caused panic and havoc and enough confusion for Jem to wrestle back control. But the smiling man did not even glance sideways. He did not, for one moment, tear his eyes away from Jem's.

'Oh come on, Jeremiah,' he said, his soft voice rippling past the shocked cries of John as he fought on with the possessed stinger. 'Shoot him if you want to, but causing a scene won't help you get back your boy, will it?'

'GIDEON! STOP!'

Gideon at last let the stinger drop and it fell back off John's body like a shed skin, dripping with the man's blood. His face was raw with puncture wounds. He sank down to his knees, fumbling for his gun in his jacket.

'Leave it there, John,' advised the man at his side.

John stared at Gideon as Gideon stared back at him, his face a hard grimace through the glass of the closed rear passenger window. The man's eyes glittered with fury and horror and he moved his hand further into his jacket.

'I said . . . ' There was a whoosh of air and the pop of a silencer and John's hand fell back. '. . . leave it,' concluded the smiling man, already pointing his gun back to Jem. John's eyes went glassy. Very slowly, he tipped forward from his knees. Then he tumbled, head first, towards the people carrier. A second later his dead face struck the closed window, a centimetre from Gideon's nose. The rattle and thud of the blood-drenched stinger followed closely behind. Gideon fell back to the far end of the seat, gasping something incoherent as the man's open eye and squashed cheek travelled slowly left along the slanting glass leaving a wide smear of blood, and came to a halt.

And still Jem held the gun steady, his gaze unwavering. 'What do you want, Yanos?' he said.

146

11

'It's no good. There's just no signal,' said Lydia, staring at Annie's mobile phone in dismay, but not surprise. She had tried her own too, but there wasn't a hint of a cell bar on it. The whole area was a nightmare for mobiles. Fish wriggled in her arms, picking up the stress in the car.

'Well, we're here,' said Annie, pulling off the road with a sharp swerve, quite unlike her usual sedate driving. 'We'll just have to go and find them and warn them ourselves. They've probably got right to the bottom of the landslip by now. I'll take the left path . . . it's all my joints can manage, I'm afraid. You go down the Devil's Chimney, Lyddy, OK?' She glanced at the girl beside her who looked pale but steady. Good in a storm, thought Annie. A coper. 'Take Fish with you. He might find them for us. Here,' she reached back into the seat behind them and grabbed a couple of fleeces, 'Luke's and Gideon's,' she said, holding them up to Fish's bemused black nose.

'Fish,' said Lydia, stroking his ears. 'SNIFF! That's LUKE and GIDEON. We want to find them, OK? FETCH—fetch Luke and Gideon!'

She had no idea whether it would work, but as she opened the car door Fish shot out and away down the path, pausing after a few seconds to check his mistress was following. 'Good boy!' she called. 'I'm just coming.' Annie, noting the darkening sky, gave her a small torch from the glove compartment. 'Thanks,' said Lydia. 'But there are no others cars. Are you sure they're here?'

'There's another place to park further down,' said Annie. 'And we have to check anyway. If we don't find them we'll think of something else—in fact, before I go down I'm going into the tea room and getting on their landline to Control.'

'Good! Of course! Why didn't I think of that?' said Lydia. 'Right—I'll go down now, OK? I'll shout if I find them . . . or . . . anything. And Fish will bark. And then I'll see you back at the car in half an hour if I don't find them first.'

148

She hurried after Fish, her heart thumping rapidly in her chest, as Annie made her way swiftly to the tea room. She still hadn't told Annie about the burglar—she had felt so shocked and sick in the car, continually seeing that poor woman's lifeless body in her mind, that she didn't feel able to add to it all with guilt. She *should* have told them all yesterday, regardless of her conviction that there was nothing to worry about. Regardless of her selfish thoughts about getting found out.

She ran along the top path calling out, 'GIDEON! GIDEON! JEM! LUKE!' After a while she remembered that even if Luke heard her he couldn't call back. But she called him anyway because it seemed wrong not to. And maybe he could make some kind of noise if he was in trouble. The atmosphere seemed to thicken as she hurried along the first steepening slant to the Devil's Chimney. It wasn't spooky exactly—she'd been coming here since she was old enough to walk; it was like her back garden—but now that she glanced up she remembered the forecast that day. Storms coming in. The air was heavy with dropping pressure. Thunder flies danced under the straggly canopy of trees which edged the cliff like a line of sightseers, bending over the mess of landslip below. A small green lizard fled from her footfalls on the path ahead. It was quiet. Nobody else seemed to be around. Now she was grasping the metal banister which led down into the chimney of rock. 'GIDEON! JEM! LUKE!' she called again, her voice blatting off the rock walls back at her. Maybe Annie was over-reacting. Maybe they were all on their way home already, after these *Control* people had contacted *them*.

Fish reached the foot of the chimney before her, his claws clipping rapidly across the stone. At the foot of it he looked up at her and whined. He turned around in a circle as if chasing his tail, but he was looking up and down the steps. 'What is it, Fish?' she said, crouching down beside him. 'Can you smell Luke? Gideon?' Fish barked twice and certainly looked as if he was agreeing, but she couldn't be sure. He wasn't some kind of wonderdog . . . just a dog.

'OK—which way?' she asked. She made a hopeful and encouraging face, bluffing herself as much as Fish. Maybe he *could* pick up the boys' scent trail. Fish immediately turned and ran out of the oppressive cave onto the outside path which wound on further down the landslip. 'Fish! Do you *know* where you're going?' she called out, hurrying after him. 'Or . . . *why*?' Fish paused, peering back at her, yapped twice again, and ran on along the path. 'OK, Wonderdog,' sighed Lydia, hoping that Annie was even now on the phone to Control being told that Jem and the twins were safe and help was on its way to her house. With luck she'd get back up top in fifteen or twenty minutes, before the storm hit. She didn't want to be on the landslip in a deluge; that was asking for trouble. 'Wait for me, Wonderdog!' she called, running faster to catch up with Fish's little furry backside.

Luke was aware of a raspy noise coming out of his throat, but in his head he heard a good old-fashioned yell of pain. He had undone the rope around his wrists and the next thing to do was get up onto all fours and climb back up the steep rock incline. Just manoeuvring his arms around beneath him had been enough to rock his pelvis and the pain that shot through his left leg knocked the breath out of him. That first bolt of pain he'd felt was nothing to this roaring agony. He lay with his head in his hands, panting and shaking until the worst of it subsided. How was he going to get himself out of here?

You're just going to have to, he told himself. *You know it. There's no point waiting around for it to get better. You'll get cold and go into shock. You have to move NOW.*

Luke gulped back some tears which had leaked out of his eyes while the pain was roaring up and down his leg. And then he decided, on balance, to let them out. He sent a few more after them, dripping down his cheeks. It was a kind of relief—the lachrymose equivalent of shouting out his distress, he realized. And he liked the word. Lachrymose. One of his favourites. Luke had always taken comfort in words, even though he could no longer speak them. OK. Time to cry his way through a journey of about . . . eight metres, he calculated. He took a deep breath, slid his hands ahead to grasp a handhold on the slanted rock, moved his good knee up to one side and then dragged his body and the bad leg along half a metre towards the dimming light above. Tears poured out of him as belt after belt of pain crashed in. He let the worst of it subside once more, sobbing it out silently, soaking the backs of his hands, and then tried again.

There was a rumble. At first he thought it was just part of the thundering in his pain centres, but then it became distinct. A rumble echoing down through the rock. Thunder. He rested his face on his hands again and remembered Jem saying, at breakfast, that there was a storm forecast in the afternoon. How long had he been down here? The light was definitely darker. But that didn't mean it was evening—just that cloud was gathering. His watch wasn't luminous; he couldn't read it at all.

He took another steadying breath, trying not to dwell on still being here when the storm struck properly. He knew this landslip well, even though his mum had not moved here until a year or so after he was 'collected' by the Cola project. He'd visited the area often enough before then to understand how this and the rest of the Undercliff on the Island had come to be the shape it was; forever sliding and tumbling into the sea. The land grew sodden with rain and then . . . just slid. Not every time it rained but often enough to make dozens of walkways redundant across the years. The lower slopes were littered with twisted wooden steps and upended benches, chunks of torn shingle path and long lost railings. Small caves and chasms opened up regularly—and were then choked shut again just as often. He knew he was in just such a chasm.

Time for more tearful fun, he realized, with a wave of sick determination. There was nothing else for it. He had seen two flashes of lightning, even from way down in here. He was not going to lie here and be washed away like a slug or buried in mud and rock and water. He wept copiously as he moved a full metre this time. The pain almost made him pass out and he could hear a shrill yapping sound in his head as his entire nervous system shrieked and his throat coughed and his nose ran. *LUKE!* called his mind. *Don't give up! Keep climbing! Don't pass out! LUKE! LUKE! LUKE!*

'LUKE!' yelled a distant voice. *Yip. Yip. Yip.* 'LUKE! Are you down *there?*'

A small circle of white light pierced the gloom and tiny clippy clawed feet danced and slid down the rock surface towards him. *Yip! Yip! Yip!* Something warm and wet moved against his face. *Yip! Yip!*

Yooray . . . thought Luke, just before he lost consciousness.

12

'You look well, Jeremiah,' said the man called Yanos with just a trace of an Eastern European accent. 'Five years older, but it hardly shows.'

Jem did not reply. He sat motionless on the plastic chair, Gideon at his side, and watched and waited.

'I'm surprised you do not want to talk,' frowned Yanos, although somehow his smile still held, like a party banner left up long after the guests have departed.

It was true that Jem had said very little as they made their way to the empty house. He had been forced to drive the Jeep—the one that Clara and John had been using, while Gideon sat in the back with the stranger, who kept a small silver handgun trained steadily on the back of Jem's neck. Jem had only said two things. First, 'Where is Luke?'—and Yanos had laughed and responded, 'I will tell you where he is when the time is right, Jeremiah. I did not kill him. You should know that.'

Gideon had wanted to pound the man's face into the window behind him and it was only the certain knowledge that he might never see Luke again if he did which held him back. He wondered if the man had even noticed his Cola power attack on John. His complete lack of reaction was something new.

'Is Clara dead?' asked Jem, secondly, his voice flat as he changed gear and overtook a bus lumbering up the hill ahead of them. 'Did you kill her?'

'I did,' said Yanos, and Jem's knuckles whitened on the steering wheel. 'It was very quick,' added Yanos. 'Merciful. Do you remember that word, Jeremiah?'

After ten minutes in the Jeep they had pulled into the overgrown driveway of a remote stone house with a dilapidated caravan in its garden. Yanos had urged them inside the building, past a swinging unlatched front door with peeling red paint, into a damp hallway and then to the right, into a small sitting room where there were three fold-out plastic chairs set out on a perishing lino floor. Gideon gulped, realizing it must all have been planned.

'Sit,' said Yanos, sweeping his hand towards the two chairs with their backs to the cracked and grimy bay window.

'Is Luke here?' asked Jem.

'Here? No! Why would I bring him here?' smiled Yanos.

Jem gritted his teeth. 'You don't know what you're messing with, Yanos,' he said. 'This is a much bigger situation than you realize. If you damage these assets, the British government will hunt you down without pause. You—your cohorts, your family . . . Your life will be over.'

'My life is already over,' said Yanos. 'And I have no family. Don't you remember? You saw to that.' There was no drama in his words. He spoke as if he was relating dry facts and as he did so he reached into a cardboard box behind his chair and Gideon wondered if he was about to bring out some instrument of torture. Instead, he brought out a can of Coke. And he handed it to Gideon. 'Here,' he said. 'Drink. It will steady you.'

Gideon stared at the can and the man waved it a little in the air in front of him, like a kindly sports coach. 'Go on,' he insisted. 'Nothing is wrong with it.'

Gideon took the Coke and pulled the ring reflexively, shaking with fear, anger and now . . . confusion.

'We can do a deal,' said Jem. 'Your problem is with me—not Gideon or his brother.'

'No—you are right, but . . . ' Yanos took out another can and opened it for himself, smiling benignly across the small brown fountain erupting from it. ' . . . I was always a poet. And when I came to kill you at Carisbrooke Castle, I saw such poetry. You . . . my old enemy, found at last . . . with your two very special "nephews". Not just brothers. *Twins.* What chance, eh? What chance? Pure poetry. It made me rewrite our final verse.' He took a sip from the drink and shook his head, putting the can on the floor. 'Gideon,' he turned his smile upon the boy, the gun in his right hand resting on his thigh. 'Shall I tell you a story about twins?'

Gideon stared at him and then also took a slug of Coke, trying to contain the ragged emotions ripping through him as he was forced to sit still.

'There were once two brothers, born two minutes apart,' said Yanos. 'Lazlo and Yanos Yakovlevicz.

Ya-kov-la-vits,' he enunciated, slowly, nodding at Gideon. 'Difficult for British people to say. Yanos and Lazlo grew up as brothers should, fighting and loving and working and . . . fighting again. One was dark and one was fair—but otherwise, they were identical. They went to school together and then they joined the army together and then they joined the special forces together. They worked well as a team because, as you will know, Gideon, being twins they could almost read each other's minds. Can you read Luke's mind, now, Gideon?'

Gideon scowled at the man. He could not read Luke's mind—not here, not now. In the same room, perhaps. Even at a distance if he could see his face, but not when he had no idea where his brother was. He was not telepathic. 'Where *is* he?' he growled.

'He is alive,' said Yanos. 'And you do not need to worry because very soon you are going to do something for me which will keep him alive.'

'Get to your *point*, Yanos,' growled Jem. 'You may think you know what's happening here—but you don't.'

'Oh—you mean the *powers*,' said Yanos, raising one eyebrow. 'Yes, I noticed that your boy here has some . . . talent. Farrier told me he is a . . . Child Of Limitless Ability. And this ability he has . . . what do you call it? Telekinesis? I guess his brother has it too. I never got to talk to him before I disabled him.'

'Is that not what you're here for?' asked Jem, disdain in his voice. 'Haven't you got some Hungarian buyer lined up? Or maybe an Afghan . . . yes, that's more your style.'

Yanos stood up and for the first time his smile fell off his face. 'You KNOW why I am here!' he shouted. 'Do not INSULT Lazlo's memory with this idiocy!'

'What . . . what happened to Lazlo?' Gideon heard himself ask. He needed to keep Yanos calm or he might lose his own slender thread of control and bring the ceiling down on the man's head. And then they'd never find Luke again.

Yanos paced back and forth for a few seconds, working his face into a less emotional shape before responding: 'Your favourite MI5 *uncle* tortured and killed him.' His eyes flicked to Gideon, to Jem and then back to Gideon. 'So you will understand, Gideon, why I am here.'

Gideon held his breath. He waited for Jem to

deny the accusation, but many seconds of silence passed. Eventually he had to ask. 'Is . . . is that true?'

Jem shook his head. 'It depends on how you look at it, Gideon.'

'You mean . . . you did . . . you killed his brother? His twin?'

'I killed Lazlo Yakovlevicz, yes,' said Jem. 'But I did not torture him. I won't say I treated him with kid gloves either. At the time the lives of a great many innocent people were resting on the information he had.'

'He knew *nothing*!' hissed Yanos, stepping closer to Jem but directing his gun towards Gideon. 'He knew *nothing* and you killed him for it!' All traces of the smile were gone and the man's face was contorted with hatred and grief, his nostrils flared and lip curled. 'You see *this*!' He flicked his left hand across the white flash through his dark hair. 'I got this when he died. This white arrived within days of his death at your hands. This is my sorrow! You took my brother. You killed him just because you *could*.'

'He knew the detonation code to the bomb,' said Jem, his voice level and insistent. 'That is how we defused it before it took out an entire Spanish marketplace. Your brother told us the code. How else would we have stopped it?'

'He did NOT know!' roared Yanos. 'He was NOT a bomber. He was a soldier.'

Jem closed his eyes and his voice grew softer. 'Yanos, please. You didn't know everything about Lazlo.'

'You don't get to say his name,' said the man and his eyes seemed to frost over, they were so cold. All the passion of his story spent, he kept his gun, still aimed at Gideon's forehead, rock steady. 'You killed him in cold blood.'

'NO!' bit back Jem. 'HOT blood, Yanos! HOT— because he was meant to be calling in. We made a deal. We let him have his phone back to make contact and bring in the ringleader. Then I saw his face and realized there *was* no deal. He was texting in the remote code to the detonator—just as the bomb disposal unit were bending over the device. Men and women and children *yards* away! I saw him do it and yes, I shot him before he could hit *Send*.'

'You *stink* of lies,' said Yanos, flatly. And then his gun moved. Suddenly and decisively. Gideon could not help it. His mind flexed and the gun flipped up out of the man's grasp and began to spin in the air above them.

Both men gasped and stared up and Jem stood, kicking the chair aside and backing away from Yanos, holding his hands up. 'Gideon!' he called. 'Stay steady. Steady now.'

But Yanos was beginning to laugh. Even as his eyes were bulging with astonishment he was laughing. 'It's all right, Gideon,' he gasped, through the laughter, 'it's just fine. I was going to give you the gun anyway. Drop it into your hand, Gideon. It's a Ruger. .22 calibre. Put it in your palm and see how it feels.'

Gideon felt sick. He had no idea what to do. All the Cola power in the world made no difference. If only Lisa or one of the other psychics were here they could get inside this madman's head and find out where Luke was, but he was just not able to.

Slap. The Ruger hit his palm and his fingers curled instinctively around it, finding the trigger. He was shivering from his toes to his teeth and the hair on his scalp was prickling but he forced his hand to be still and steady. He pointed it at Yanos and the man's grim smile returned. 'I can kill you now,' Gideon said. 'You saw what I did to Farrier.

You saw that. You know I will kill you.'

'I know you *can* kill me,' said Yanos. 'And in truth, Gideon, it doesn't matter to me if I never leave this room. Now it's all about what matters to *you.*'

Gideon clenched his fingers and gritted his teeth. 'Where's Luke? Tell me or I'll shoot you.'

'And then you'll never know,' said Yanos.

Gideon changed the angle of the gun. 'I can shoot you more than once,' he warned, the words cold in his mouth. Torture was suddenly perfectly do-able.

'Ah, no—you cannot,' said Yanos. 'There is only one bullet. But you must shoot, Gideon, before we can get anywhere. I will tell you where Luke is. I will even drive you to him and help you retrieve him, but first you must do something for me. You are a twin. You understand.'

'What are you *talking* about?' breathed Gideon.

'Do you have any idea what it is like to lose your brother, I wonder?' asked Yanos, tilting his head to one side.

Gideon nodded. The months of pain that had followed Luke's apparent death were months he would never forget.

'Then you know how I suffer,' said Yanos. 'And you know what you must do. Twin for twin. It's very simple. I want you to shoot his killer.'

13

A prickling sensation on his scalp woke Luke. At first he thought it must be Fish licking his hair, but the little dog was a few feet away, behind Lydia who was lying on her front, head down, a little way above him. 'Luke! How did you get down here? What happened?'

Luke went to move his hands and then remembered she couldn't read his signs anyway, so didn't bother. The throbbing in his left leg warned him of more pain to come as soon as he tried to reach her. His scalp prickled again. It meant something—something important—but he couldn't remember what.

'Sorry,' said Lydia. 'I keep forgetting you can't speak. But we've got to get you out of here. It's raining like mad and we're on a really crumbly

166

part of the landslip. It feels dangerous. Fish wants us to get out of here yesterday!' As if to dramatize her words there was another flash and a rumble of thunder and Fish let off another volley of anxious yips.

There was no point waiting to explain. Luke knew he had to get going. If he just lay here he would be putting Lydia and Fish in danger too. He began to crawl again, dragging his bad leg and feeling the sweat and tears springing out of him once more. It was horrible enough before, but worse in the full glare of Lydia's torch.

'Oh no, Luke—you're really hurt, aren't you?' she said, her words flattened by her awkward angle and her anxiety. '*Damn.*' She tried to help him, grabbing his arm and crawling backwards up through the shallow slanting cave, but he shook her off, gritting his teeth and shutting his eyes. Then something hot snaked down his spine from the prickling on his scalp—and suddenly the pain in his leg eased down just a notch. Enough for him to draw in a lungful of determination and crawl harder. As he emerged, thirty seconds later, into the dim afternoon light, a guttural croak of pain was escaping his throat. He flopped onto the thick green grass which almost hid the cave entrance and registered some amazement. That was very possibly the first real noise that had got out of his voicebox in two years.

Lydia and Fish bent over him with identical expressions of concern, although Luke noted with some relief that Lydia's tongue wasn't hanging out. 'You've broken your leg, I think,' she said. He nodded, puffing out. 'I have no idea how you just managed to get out of there,' she added. She glanced up the cracked path to the high cliffs above them. 'And I have no idea how we'll get you up to the top.'

Luke had no idea either. He was spent. He lay there, the air shuddering in and out of his lungs and rain washing his face, wishing he could tell them both just to go. A small fast river of rainwater was already winding across this barely-trodden passage through the ivy and brambles, carrying silt and tiny pebbles and leaf litter with it. The whole area was unstable. His telekinetic radar was sensing movement. Big movement. He waved a weary hand at Lydia as she peered unhappily at his bruised and swollen left leg. *Go! GO!*

'I can't leave you down here!' she said, staring

agitatedly around her. 'I could try to send Wonderdog here back to your mum. Fish might be able to find her.'

Luke's eyebrows rose in astonishment. His mum was here?

'Yes, your mum's up top,' said Lydia. 'She went to the tea rooms to phone for help. Oh, Luke, something's badly wrong. We found a body in the woods . . . it was . . . that woman who was helping to protect you and Gideon. Clara . . . ?'

Luke squeezed his eyes shut as the worst case scenario grew horribly real in his head. Whoever had attacked him was going after Gideon and Jem too. Was it John? The new MI5 guy? Or had he been attacked too?

A scratchy, grating kind of low rumble interrupted his unhappy thoughts and his eyes sprang open again. Lydia had snatched Fish to her and the little dog was whimpering. 'Oh no,' she moaned. 'That was a slip. I know the sound. Luke—we've got to get you out of here. Somehow, you've got to get up!'

Luke tried to sit up but the pain was back again, as if someone had set fire to the very bones in his legs. His head spun. He waved again at Lydia.

169

GO! Go ON! Get OUT of here! She understood him well enough and she wanted to go, but she was anchored down with fear for him.

'I'm not just *leaving* you here!' she argued. 'How could I?'

Luke felt a bitter smile crease his face. Of all the times for a girl to prove him wrong . . . If she stayed she could end up being buried alive alongside him. But she wasn't going anywhere; she was holding his hand and staring around, trying to work out how to save him. It might have gone on that way for ever—or until a landslide got them—but then, to his amazement, there came the sound of footfalls. Heavy ones. Heading in their direction. Three people.

'Over here!' yelled Lydia, her voice shrill through the patter of the thickening rain. 'Quick! Help! Over here!'

Three people came. A woman and a man, both in their twenties, thought Luke, and an older guy who seemed pretty fit despite his white hair. They crouched down looking worried.

'I think he's broken his leg,' said Lydia. 'He needs a stretcher . . . but we can't wait here. It's too dangerous. We have to move him.'

'Yes,' said the white-haired man, scanning the darkening gully around them. 'There's not much time.'

'Luke, I'm so sorry,' said Lydia, leaning in to him. 'This is going to hurt you so much but we can't leave you here. Even an air ambulance could never reach you.'

The white-haired man was touching his leg gently. 'It may not be a break,' Luke heard him say. 'It might only be a sprain.'

Luke felt his leg go warm and the tingle was back on his scalp. Of *course* . . . he began to lose consciousness again but this time he went on a tiny boost of hope. Lisa or Paulina Sartre were dowsing him, tracing his whereabouts remotely from hundreds of miles away at Fenton Lodge. And maybe Mia had found a way to connect with them and heal him remotely too . . . *it was going to be OK.* He blacked out.

The white-haired man fixed Lydia with very blue eyes and said, 'Now is the time, while he's out.' He then took charge, organizing them into a human stretcher, getting Lydia and the young couple to help him carefully lift Luke, keeping him as straight and supported as possible as they carried him up along the steep, overgrown paths.

Lydia's heart was thundering with panic that one of them would stumble, in the downpour, on such treacherous paths and Luke would wake up screaming at any moment, but his eyes remained closed as if he was in a blissful sleep. They came to a tight curve on the path which led them up beneath a glowering overhang of cliff face. And then something extraordinary happened. The man with white hair suddenly shouted 'STOP!' and they all froze. A slithering, scratching rumble began to break through the hiss of the rain and Lydia felt her insides clench in horror. Fish held back behind them, whining. They were standing in the epicentre of a landslip hot spot and a landslip was happening NOW.

As the young couple stared around in terror the white-haired man grabbed Luke's head and shouted, 'LUKE!' Luke's eye's shot wide open and his hand flew up, pointing at the rocky outcrop above them at exactly the moment a large crack opened up in it, showering dirt and pebbles down upon them. Lydia's eyes were transfixed upon the several tonnes of cliff face now hanging just above their heads . . . with *no connection* to the land mass behind. She could see chinks of pale stormy sky through the fissure. They should all be pulped beneath the rock fall by now and yet here they still were, frozen on the path while the broken cliff hovered in thin air.

'Walk now,' said the man with the white hair. 'Keep calm and walk on.'

Luke's eyes remained locked open and his hand trained on the impossible hovering cliff above them but somehow everyone else got moving. They made it to the next turn in the path, Fish now running ahead, and then Luke let his hand drop and closed his eyes again. An incredible crash and roar shook the air and the ground all around them and the woman screamed. But they had moved past the slippage and were on solid ground now. Five minutes later they reached the top and the grassy lawn by the tea rooms where Annie fell sobbing upon Luke and had to be held off as he was revived with water and covered in a rug.

'Control are sending help!' she whispered to Luke as his eyes fluttered open.

Where's Gideon? he signed, feeling just a little stronger.

'I don't know,' said Annie, wiping tears off her face. 'But Jem is with him—I'm sure of it. And whatever happens, Jem will keep him safe.'

14

How good was he? This was Gideon's main thought. Just how *good* was he?

'Go on, Gideon. You can make it quick,' said Yanos. 'He won't have to suffer. He would have been dead by now anyway, so you could say he's had a bonus twenty-four hours thanks to you.'

'Thanks to *me*?' The words came out dry and raspy through gritted teeth. The Ruger shook in his hand, pointing still at Yanos.

'Well, yes,' smiled Yanos. 'I was planning to kill him yesterday, at the castle. He was right there in my sights in the Great Hall. I was up in the roof space all ready to party.'

Gideon's mouth dropped open as he remembered Lisa's warning. *Stay out of the Great Hall.* And *the dark twin has death for you.* WHY hadn't he told Jem?

Why had he not taken Lisa seriously? He'd been so worried that their holiday would be cut short that he just hadn't bothered after nothing happened in the Great Hall—and now here he was, with a dark twin. And the dark twin definitely had death for Jem. And maybe for Luke and himself too.

'I was just about to pull my trigger when I saw your face, Jeremiah,' Yanos was saying. 'I saw this extraordinary thing. I saw you were watching your boys and you had *love* in your eyes.'

'Tosh!' said Jem, gripping the back of the plastic chair. 'They're just assets. It was my job to nursemaid them for a week, that's all. Wiping the noses of a pair of teenagers does not get me dewy-eyed and paternal, let me tell you. So just get your job done. Take the gun back and end it now. Gideon's a lousy shot, he's more likely to hit you than me even if he *does* aim at me.'

Gideon winced at Jem's words, but still pointed the gun steadily at Yanos.

'No,' said Yanos, shaking his head slowly and watching his enemy closely. 'You care about them—I can see this even now. I see it in the sweat on your brow, Jeremiah. The tough man; a British operative of the toughest MI5 steel. What has happened to you? You *care*. And this is what has brought us here today. I wanted to get revenge on you, my friend. You tortured my brother into giving you information and then you betrayed him. You didn't leave him a shred of honour. My people believe he was a traitor; that he willingly sold them out. So—kill you? Yes, I could do that. Easily. But . . . ' Yanos licked his lips and glanced across at Gideon, his smile deepening to something awful. 'Why not take something you care about first? I was thinking of killing them both in front of you but then I thought, no . . . corruption is better. So—this boy gets to keep *his* twin brother, only if he first becomes a killer. So what do you say, Gideon? What are you thinking?'

'I'm thinking,' said Gideon, moving the gun. 'How good am I?'

'Good is an abstract idea,' said Yanos. 'Is it good to kill a man? You would think not. But is it good to kill one man to save another? It can be.'

Gideon weighed the gun in his palm. He knew Yanos was telling the truth about the bullet; his telekinetic sense of mass, shape, density and movement told him this. He and Luke had an instinctive understanding of the physical world

177

around them and all its properties. He also knew that Yanos would never tell him where Luke was if he shot him in the leg—not even if he and Jem tortured him together. He didn't need ESP to recognize that the man was past caring, possessed with a need for revenge which blotted out every other desire.

'You are a good boy, I can see that,' Yanos was continuing. 'It is hard for you. You are good— but sometimes the good must be bad. You cannot sacrifice your brother for this man, can you? Not knowing what he has done. What he *is*. Kill him and keep your twin. That is what a good brother should do.'

'You don't understand,' said Gideon. 'I have to be *very* good. And I think . . . ' He swung the gun round and pointed it directly towards the middle of Jem's forehead. ' . . . I am.'

He pulled the trigger.

15

Jem hit the dusty floor like a felled tree, flat on his back—a dark red dot on his brow and his eyes already shut. In the silence that followed the shot, Gideon clutched the gun with both hands, his face a mask, and then opened the cartridge chamber to peer inside.

'Sorry, my young friend,' said Yanos. 'I spoke the truth. Only one bullet.'

'Only one,' said Gideon, closing the cartridge chamber and pocketing the gun.

'I am impressed,' said Yanos, his voice hushed. 'I did not think I would convince you so fast.' He walked towards the body.

'Forget him now!' said Gideon. 'You take me to Luke. You take me RIGHT NOW.'

Yanos turned away from Jem and tilted his head, considering.

'Very well,' he said. 'You did what I asked of you. Now I will fulfil my promise. Come.' He stepped out of the room and into the corridor without a backward glance.

Gideon paused and looked down at Jem's face. 'Jem . . . I'm so sorry,' he said. 'Forgive me.' A rumble of thunder outside seemed to answer '*Not a hope in hell*'.

He followed Yanos outside as the rain which had threatened for the past half hour began to fall, and opened the passenger door of the people carrier. Yanos had taken the ignition key from Jem as soon as they had arrived . . . just fifteen minutes ago. Gideon could not believe what had happened in so short a space of time. He knew he would never be the same again.

'Where is Luke?' he grunted, climbing into the passenger seat and putting on his seatbelt as a reflex as Yanos slammed the driver's door shut.

'Not far from where you last saw him,' said Yanos. 'I disabled him and then threw him in a cavern further down the landslip. If you had continued your search instead of trying to reach Control you might well have found him. But I know

Jeremiah . . . correction, I *knew* Jeremiah . . . too well. He would call in Control before any other action. I even knew which phone box he would make for. Some operatives are extremely predictable.'

Yanos put the vehicle into gear and drove it out onto the road, setting off the windscreen wipers and dashing runnels of grey water to left and right . 'We will take a different route in,' he said. 'By now your Control people may have worked out something is amiss, with no operatives at all calling in and no camera or audio feeds working.' He sniggered and shook his head. 'And these people are protecting *you*? The biggest assets in the UK? In my country this could never happen. You would *never* be left vulnerable.'

'Yeah, I bet,' said Gideon. 'Never let outside a concrete bunker.'

The man shrugged. 'You are not a normal human, Gideon. None of your friends are. You cannot expect a normal life. Your country is soft at its core to allow you what you have.'

'You know about us?' Gideon was shocked, even though he had been warned before today that Cola intel had surely leaked across the entire planet by now.

He shrugged again. 'I do not care about you.'

'Do you care about anything?' Gideon closed his eyes as he saw, again, Jem falling back in the dust. 'Now that he's dead.'

'Nothing much,' said Yanos. '*Where I must I go and what I must I bear.* Thom Gunn. One of my favourite poets. A man who understands an empty soul.'

A chopping sound beat through the air above them.

'Ah—company! So soon,' laughed Yanos as the blurry reflection of a low flying military helicopter flashed across the wet road ahead of them. 'And I thought we would have more time to get to know one another.'

'I never want to know you,' said Gideon.

'And now you will not.' Yanos ground the gears and swerved off the main road into a winding lane completely covered by a canopy of trees stretching across from either side. 'I must leave you here.'

'NO!' yelled Gideon. 'You said you would take me to LUKE! Don't you dare run out on me now!'

The car lurched to a halt on a small passing point in the road. Yanos killed the engine and then turned to peer at Gideon quizzically. 'Your people are here. They will find him. They probably already have. Farrier switched off all their tracking technology but surely they have found a way to switch it back on again.'

'What if they *haven't*?' Gideon grabbed the man's wrist. 'You said you *threw* him down. What if he's hurt and lost and in danger? You TELL me where he is.' The central locking on the vehicle clunked without Gideon even directing his thought through his eyes. Outside there was a flash of lightning and another rumble of thunder behind the endless percussion of the rain.

Yanos pushed the unlock button and the electrics obeyed him. Five seconds later Gideon was chasing him through the rain. He would have had no hope of keeping up with the man if he hadn't been pulling every piece of woodland his mind could seize upon into his quarry's path. But Yanos dodged and weaved with an athlete's reflexes, and only stopped when a metal five-bar gate suddenly lifted off its post and wrapped itself around him like a toffee paper. Then he stood still within its hot curve and turned to stare at Gideon with amazement.

'You are astonishing!' he called.

'TAKE ME TO LUKE!' bawled Gideon as he

reached the man. He was soaked through and his chest ached with effort while his head buzzed with the power of the telekinesis he was forcing through it.

'OK! OK! I will show you where he is and then I go,' said Yanos, twisting out of the weird embrace of the bent gate and running into the field it led into. 'I find I do not care to die today after all . . .' called back the man as Gideon caught up with him. 'Not while there is such wonder in the world.'

They ran down a steep meadow slope, at the edge of the grass where hedgerows and small trees hid them from the two helicopters which were now criss-crossing the area under search. Gideon felt his insides lurch. He so badly wanted rescue; for Control to parachute in and capture this terrible human being he was running with; to make it all OK. But he could not be sure they had found Luke—not if what Yanos said was true and Farrier had ruined all the tracking connections to the chips in their clothes. Lisa—or Paulina Sartre— might have dowsed Luke, but that wasn't certain. Nothing was. And knowing what he knew of this man, Control getting involved might end any hope he had of finding his brother. Yanos seemed to be working on some random sense of honour now, but for how long? He was clearly a very changeable man. Control might wreck everything for Luke.

'There!' said Yanos, stopping abruptly. 'Your brother is down there.'

Gideon stared after the man's pointed finger and then back into his smiling face. 'Down *there*?' he echoed, horrified.

'Well, he *was* down there,' said Yanos, holding on to a young oak tree to keep from sliding down the slope into a treacherous chasm lined with collapsed trees and straining undergrowth—the far edge of the land slip. Even as he gaped, appalled, Gideon saw, through the rain, a small outcrop suddenly slide away down the slope with a hiss of loose clay and shingle.

'You can probably reach him if you try,' said Yanos. 'He won't have gone anywhere. I broke his leg. And tied his hands. But look—if you jump you can ride the avalanche down to him! And so I have fulfilled my promise. I will leave you now. I am done.'

'Oh no, you're not,' said Gideon. 'You *don't* get to just walk away. You don't get to come here and rip our lives apart and then just *walk away*.'

'Ah, but I do,' said Yanos, already stepping away from the edge. 'You will not kill again today, Gideon. You do not have the taste for it. Not twice in one day.'

'Who said anything about killing?' said Gideon and a second later the young tree convulsed into life and dragged Yanos into its branches.

The man gave a shout of surprise as he was swept off his feet, and began to struggle, unable to believe that mere branches could hold him. But the branches didn't just hold him; they contracted around him like molten metal, sap boiling inside them as the heat of Gideon's rage bent them exactly as he wished. Yanos's eyes bulged and the last trace of smile was wiped off his features.

Behind him Gideon heard the chopper land, then the chatter of radio communication, shouts, the thud of men running. Still he held Yanos imprisoned in branches, his arms and legs snagged and pinched, and a runner of ivy twisted up the tree trunk, across the branches that held his hips and up his torso to his neck. It grew around his throat, tiny tendrils waving frenziedly—and began to tighten.

'GIDEON!' yelled a voice he vaguely recognized. 'GIDEON! STOP!'

The woody rope of ivy strained tight and trembled and Yanos made a rasping noise, his eyes rolling back into his head. Gideon wanted to snap his neck. Only the last thin shred of his former self was stopping him. He saw poor Jem, falling back into the dust. This disgusting man had forced him to do that. Forced him by using his love for Luke and his fear of losing him again. Yanos deserved to die, mangled like a broken doll, here in the tree in the rain.

'GIDEON!'

Arms grabbed his shoulders.

'GIDEON!' It was Chambers, the head of the Cola project. 'Leave him, Gideon! We have him. He's not going anywhere. We have Luke too. Luke is safe! It's over. Luke is safe.'

These final three words were what cut the power. Gideon sagged backwards and Chambers caught him and lowered him to his knees on the wet ground. Four or five operatives in black jackets and helmets moved in on Yanos. Chambers gripped Gideon's shoulders and stared at the tree; its branches twisted into a cage around the boy's semi-conscious foe. It was raining hot sap to the ground, the drops popping and steaming in the soaked grass.

'It's OK, Gideon,' said Chambers. 'It's all OK now.'

Gideon turned to stare into Chambers's familiar face and saw that it was awash with concern and . . . not a little fear. 'It's not OK,' he mumbled, feeling numb now as the words faltered in his mouth, 'It will never be OK again. You don't know what I've done.'

16

They let him speak to Annie via a satellite phone in a small armoured truck that Chambers had commandeered to drive back to the deserted house. Until he heard Annie say his brother was fine, Gideon had been unable to speak a further word. The horror of what he had to tell just locked down his throat. Like Luke, he was mute.

As soon as he heard Annie confirm that Luke was with her now, safe and conscious, and they were just leaving for Newport under armed guard, heading for the hospital, Gideon's throat unlocked and shuddering breaths came from it.

'Are you all right, love?' asked Annie. 'We were so worried about you. This—oh this has been such a horrible day. Gideon? Talk to me . . . '

'I'm OK,' said Gideon in a choked voice, sending

the car indicator to the left with an instinctive mind push, so Chambers would know which way to go. 'But . . . Annie . . . I had to do something terrible.'

'What, Gideon?' whispered Annie, tears in her voice.

He couldn't answer. A sob was crouching in his throat, blocking any hope of talk.

'What did you do, Gideon?'

'He'll ring you back, Annie,' said Chambers, pulling into the driveway of the deserted house. He ended the call and turned to face Gideon as he pulled the car to a halt. Behind them two other black special ops vehicles closed in.

'OK, Gideon,' said Chambers. 'Is there anything I need to know before we go in there? I think I can guess what we're going to find.'

Gideon shook his head and got out of the car. All he could see was that little red dot on Jem's forehead.

The dust rising as he hit the floor.

How good am I?

He felt the gun in his pocket.

How good was I?

'There was only one bullet,' he told Chambers as

they stepped back into the damp house. The rain had stopped now and sun was shafting through the window of the room he had last seen Jem in.

'One bullet,' repeated Chambers, turning to look at Gideon with an expression of such compassion, Gideon realized that he knew. Or thought he knew.

'In this,' said Gideon, taking the gun from his jeans pocket. Chambers stared at the weapon but did not take it from him. Just beyond the door to the right Gideon could see Jem's feet in the stout walking boots he'd put on that morning for their fun climb down the Devil's Chimney.

'I had to shoot him or lose Luke,' said Gideon.

'I know,' said Chambers, gently. 'Yanos Yakovlevicz was an appalling man. I'm so sorry, Gideon.'

'You don't know,' said Gideon. '*I* don't know yet. It hit dead centre of the forehead. But I don't know how good I was.'

Chambers frowned a little. 'Gideon—if it went through his head, point blank range . . . there's no way he's survived.'

'It didn't go through.' Gideon released the cartridge chamber and upended the Ruger.

'What?' Chambers looked confused.

'It didn't go through,' said Gideon. 'It just

touched him—just to make a mark and knock him out. And then . . . '

Chambers was gaping at him now, his eyes creased behind his rimless lenses, as if holding off pure astonishment. 'And then . . . ?'

'I called it back,' said Gideon.

He tipped a single bullet onto his palm.

Chambers opened and closed his mouth twice and then turned and ran to the body in the living room. Jem had rolled over onto his side. A widening bruise marked a target shape around the red blood blister on his forehead. He groaned as Chambers knelt over him and took his pulse.

Suddenly the room was full of people, collecting Jem on a stretcher and bearing him away. Jem was conscious. He was talking. He was saying something to Gideon who stood like a pillar of concrete, too numb with delayed shock to feel the surges of relief and joy which were crashing into him, somewhere far away.

'Gideon,' croaked Jem. 'Gideon! I forgive you!'

17

It was only as Luke was being carefully loaded into the ambulance that The Real World of Lydia Carr came back. For the past couple of hours she had been living in some kind of parallel universe of dead bodies, lost friends, panicky scrambles around a dissolving undercliff, thunder, lightning, caves, heaven-sent rescuers and—most parallel of all—a boy who could not speak, but *could* change the laws of physics while barely conscious.

Annie got into the ambulance with Luke and two men—one obviously a paramedic and the other from this 'Control' place she'd heard about so recently. Several other 'Control' people were swarming over the lawn area around the Smuggler's Haven tea room, along with police, who had closed the café and shepherded away anyone attempting to arrive by foot or by car. The young couple who had helped rescue Luke were being interviewed over a checked red tablecloth inside the café; the white-haired man who had been so assured during the rescue seemed to have gone, though. Now Annie was beckoning to her from the ambulance.

'Are you coming, Lyddy?' She looked flushed and worn out but also full of energy-giving love for Luke, whose hand she was clasping firmly as he lay back, dozing in the happy realm of morphine.

Lydia squeezed Fish in her arms and shook her head. 'No—for one thing I don't think they let dogs ride in ambulances, and for another, they're waiting to interview me.' She shrugged back towards a man and a woman from Control just behind her. 'Call me as soon as you know how Gideon is,' she said. And at the thought of the missing brother The Real World Of Lydia Carr suddenly fell onto her head, like a flop of cold water from an upturned bucket.

'Oh my God!' she screamed. 'MATTY!'

Annie turned out to be formidable, even while heading off in an ambulance. 'You will take her to her little brother NOW!' she yelled at the man and woman from Control. 'No debriefing until she's back with her brother! You understand? Or

Chambers will hear about it!'

There was a terse discussion between the man and the woman and then they both nodded and stepped towards Lydia. 'OK, love,' said the woman, a gym-fit blonde in the regulation black jacket and trousers. 'Where's his school? We'll pick him up and then interview you at home.'

Lydia leapt into the back seat of a dark green Mercedes 4 x 4 and bellowed directions to the school. It really wasn't far but a cold terror gripped her insides because it was thirty minutes past his collection time already. Someone would have taken him back inside and phoned home, or walked him back there themselves, or just asked the question 'Where's your mum, Matthew?' once too often and he would have finally begun to cry and tell the truth.

And even if he was just waiting, as usual, being brave, how could she protect their fragile lives now? With all these official 'Control' people and the Island police teeming around them. *Why* did she have to get involved with Gideon and Luke? WHY?

You didn't. They saved your life, remember.

She felt as if her insides were corroding with acid terror by the time they reached Matty's school. She threw herself out of the car, leaving Fish behind, and sprinted to the gate. It was standing open and the playground was empty. 'MATTY!' she yelled, covering the concrete at speed and swiping her head from side to side. 'MATTY! Are you HERE?'

'It's all right, Lydia,' said a kindly voice. It was Sandra Bilk, one of the dinner ladies she knew well. 'He's gone home already.'

'Home?' Lydia stared at her, astonished. 'By himself? You let him go by himself?'

'No, love,' smiled Sandra. 'Your mum picked him up.'

In the back of the car Lydia sat for a moment in a shock so profound she could not speak. Eventually she croaked out her address to the Control people and they drove her there with the occasional concerned glance back at her.

At the house everything looked normal, except the front door was open. As soon as they were out of the car Fish began barking with great excitement and tore up the path to the house. 'Lydia? Are you OK?' asked the Control woman and Lydia blinked and tried to get her head straight as she clasped the little rusted iron curls of the front gate. She had been terrified of these people coming back and finding out her secret. And now they were here. And now she had no idea where to pin her feelings. Hope, panic, confusion—and more emotions she couldn't even name—were hitting her in waves as she stared at the front door.

'Lyddy!' Matty raced out of it, his little face a picture of uncomplicated joy. 'Lyddy! She's back! Mummy's back!'

A slim woman with fair hair stepped out into the garden and smiled at her. 'Hello Lyddy,' said Mum. She took in the two strangers at her daughter's side and then added 'How was your day?'

Gideon cried when he finally got to Luke. He didn't care that Annie could see—in fact he needed the hug she gave him while he let it all out, sitting in the private ward of the hospital with Control people posted along the corridor outside.

He found, oddly, that he was able to tell Luke about everything he'd done much more easily using only his hands. As Luke lay back on his pillows, his leg already in traction and his eyes looking oddly large without his glasses, Gideon signed the story of their fear when they realized Luke had gone: about the desperate hunt for him, the car crashing over the edge of the road, the stinger attack on John Farrier and his eventual death, the kidnap and the derelict house, and the terrible choice he'd had to make to shoot Jem.

I can't believe it worked, he signed, and Luke signed back, *Of course it worked. You are the best telekinetic in the world.* And that's when the tears had come. Annie had followed enough of his signing and body language and heard enough from Chambers by now to know more or less what had happened.

'You *are* amazing,' she told him, handing him a hanky. 'Such courage! In the face of all that fear and panic you took control of a *bullet*! You saved Jem's life, without a doubt. If you hadn't done what you did, that awful man would have just killed him in front of you. And then to capture him afterwards— Gideon, that was extraordinary!'

'But,' he spoke aloud now, 'how could I do that? That thing with the stinger? That thing with the tree. I wanted to *kill* them. I really did. That's not *me*! I'm . . . I'm the comedy Cola. I'm the one who makes farty noises and winds up Lisa and eats too much chocolate. I don't want to *kill people*. What happened?'

Luke shook his brother's shoulder, made him look, and then signed, *You DIDN'T kill anyone. All the death is down to Yanos. Not you. You SAVED Jem. You even stopped short of killing Yanos. That is REAL strength.*

'*I* would have killed him,' said Annie. She gave Luke and Gideon a slow nod. 'Without a twinge of remorse, either, for threatening you both so coldly. For killing poor Clara, too. But you did so well today, Gideon. I could not be prouder of you. He messed with you both and you sent him packing. Just forget him now.'

After both brothers had been given assorted checks by Cola Project medical staff, Chambers came back to fill them in, so forgetting Yanos wasn't an option for the short term.

'Yanos wasn't coming for you at all,' he said, sitting next to Annie in the seats beside Luke's bed while Gideon perched on the end of it. 'He didn't even *know* about the Colas until he made contact with Farrier. Farrier,' he grimaced, 'apparently owed him a few favours. Yanos had evidence of some corruption Farrier had been involved in some years back; that's how he got to him and . . . to us. But he was after Jem, pure and simple. Revenge.'

He shook his head. 'Yanos used to be a trusted ally, believe it or not. Worked with British operatives on a number of anti-terrorism missions. But his brother Lazlo . . . he wasn't so steady. The truth is, Lazlo sold out. Jem *did* kill him, but there was really no choice. He was about to activate a bomb in a crowded place with his phone. It was a split second call for Jem. He had to shoot.'

'So—surely Yanos could see what had happened,' said Gideon, spitting the man's name out with distaste.

'He could,' said Chambers. 'But his brother's death broke his mind, I think. He didn't want to reason things out; didn't want to look at what his beloved twin really *was*. The only thing keeping him going was revenge.'

Annie suddenly glanced up. 'Speaking of brothers—did Lydia get back to Matthew? Are they being looked after? She really has had the most shocking day.'

'Lydia's being debriefed at home with her little brother and her mum,' said Chambers.

Luke's and Gideon's mouths dropped open in an identical fashion.

'With her *mum*?' asked Gideon.

'Yes,' said Chambers, standing. 'Naturally. She is under eighteen, you know! All the usual protocols will apply, of course, in making sure your Cola status isn't compromised.'

'It won't be!' said Gideon, hurriedly. 'She never saw us do anything, did she, Luke?'

Luke shook his head fervently.

'I don't think you need to worry about Lydia,' added Annie, quickly. 'We're very good friends and I would certainly know if she had learned the boys' secret.'

'Well—we'll see,' said Chambers. 'Now—I'm off to see Jem. Gideon, would you like to come with me?'

Gideon gulped. Then he stood and nodded and followed Chambers along a pale cream corridor to another side ward where Jem lay in bed looking rather impatient.

'Will you just sign me out of here, Chambers?' he said, as soon as they opened the door. 'All I've got is a bruised forehead, for crying out loud! Oh—hi, Gideon.' Jem gave a little wave and a grin and then went on, 'Seriously, Chambers—there's work to do. We need to get on to John Farrier's story. We need to find out what weak link let that man into the Project. We need to nail down all the—'

201

'Shut up, Jem,' said Chambers. 'Or I'll have them sedate you.'

Jem opened his mouth to protest and then glanced again at Gideon, saw his stricken face, and knew enough to be quiet.

'How—how are you?' asked Gideon, eyeing the target-shaped bruise on Jem's brow.

'Minor headache—paracetamol,' shrugged Jem. 'Did I really tell that man you were a lousy shot?'

Gideon smiled and nodded.

'I am . . . just amazed,' said Jem. 'When I came round and felt the bump and realized you were gone . . . I just couldn't believe it. You really held the bullet back with your mind?'

Gideon nodded again. 'I didn't know for sure that it would work, but I knew that if I didn't pretend, he'd just shoot you anyway. Jem . . . the look you gave me when I took aim. I—' he gulped again and took a steadying breath. 'You were so . . . *understanding*. Right then when you must have known I was about to shoot and there was no hope.'

'It was not your fault, Gideon. You got caught up in some of my unfinished business and it was deeply unfair on you,' said Jem. 'All you ever wanted was a week's holiday!'

'I suppose that's over now,' sighed Gideon. 'Well . . . at least we got half of it.'

'No,' said Jem, sitting up. 'You are going to have the rest of your holiday.'

Chambers raised an eyebrow.

'No—look at it,' said Jem. 'The place will be swarming with police and press, yes—but we can control that. I imagine you're already feeding a good cover story to the media . . . ? So . . . let them have three more days at Bonchurch. All the security tech will be up and running again by now—MI5's finest are already here. C'mon. Give the kid the rest of his holiday!'

Gideon smiled hopefully at Chambers and watched the man's other brow go up alongside the first.

'Sometimes,' said Chambers, 'I surprise myself.' He sighed. He nodded. 'Two more days!' he said. '*Two.*'

After the Control people had gone there was a very long silence at the kitchen table. Lydia stared at her clay-stained fingers, wrapped around a mug of tepid tea, and tried to think of anything at all to say. Outside in the back garden, Matty was running round and round with Fish and a new ball.

Eventually, Mum broke the silence.

'Well . . . that was . . . unexpected.' Her voice sounded so . . . *normal.* Just like it used to before Dad died. Just as if time had been flipped back.

'Unexpected, yes,' said Lydia.

'Lyddy . . .'

Lydia sniffed. She raised her hands and her shoulders. *Well?*

'Lyddy . . . I hardly know what to say.'

Lydia stared at her. Her mother's face was different. It was no longer filled with lines and hollows and her brown eyes were not rimmed with red. But there was a hesitancy around her mouth and her throat bobbed again and again. Her hair was longer, held back in a loose plait. Her clothes were clean and smelt vaguely of spices. She was like a being from another world. If a silver shaft of light had suddenly opened up and ported her back to a different dimension, Lydia would not have been surprised.

'Well,' said Lydia, 'how about telling me where you've been? Or—no—how about how two weeks turned into five months? Or . . . I don't know . . . how much you missed Matty and me?' Rage was building up inside her. Her very ribs were shaking with it.

'Oh, Lyddy—I *did*—I really did miss you both! I can't explain . . . ' Now her mother's hands took hold of hers. 'I was in such a dark place. I really forgot who I was for a while. But I was with some people who looked after me well. It's just that . . . they didn't realize I'd left you two behind. I believed, for a long time, that you were back with Mrs Hatfield. I sort of had a mental mindslip.'

'Mrs Hatfield? The foster mother?' repeated Lydia, appalled. 'You know we hated it there!'

'I know, honey, I know,' said Mum, tears now welling in her eyes. 'But she wasn't cruel to you or anything, was she? It was just such a hard time— of course you hated it. But I thought you'd still be better off with her than me. I told you, didn't I? I told you to go to her if I didn't come back in a few days.'

Lydia blinked and remembered. Yes. Mum *had* told her that in her note. She had even put the phone number of Mrs Hatfield on the corkboard in the kitchen. Lydia had ignored it completely.

'So . . . I thought you were with her,' went on Mum. 'I got to this retreat in Wales and then I just waited for all the greyness to go again so I could come back when I was some good to you. I—I didn't even really know how long I was there.'

'So what changed?' said Lydia. 'What brought you back?'

'Your dad,' said Mum.

Lydia stared at her sharply. Just when she seemed—really—to be quite together again . . . this?

'Mum! Dad is DEAD! Remember? Narrow lane! Oncoming lorry! Dead Dad!' She smacked her hands down on the table top. 'You remember REALITY, don't you?'

'Yes, sweetheart, I know he's dead,' said Mum, and there was something in her voice which ignited the tiniest spark of hope in Lydia. 'But he's always with us. I know this now. A couple of days ago I had a really vivid dream. There was a girl . . . blonde . . . a bit stroppy. She . . . well, she kind of told me off, really. Said I should get my ar—well, my act together—and go home. I didn't recognize her but then she left and your dad arrived and told me it was time to pick up and get on. And ever since, I've been getting this little tickle-tickle feeling in my hair, as if he's touching my head and reminding me. You know, I *was* getting better anyway—but part of me was afraid of coming back and finding you hated me and would never see me again. That social services would lock me out of your lives for ever. I was hesitating for about a month—and then . . . that strange tickling and the dream of your dad and now . . . Now I am back. And if you can still possibly have me, I will *never* leave you alone again.'

Lydia stood up and went to the window. Matty was still running around with Fish, full of fun. 'It's been so hard for Matty,' she said.

'Look at this place,' said Mum getting up and gazing around the room. 'You've held it all together. You've kept going—I don't know how but you have. You are your father's daughter, and no mistake. It's been hard for Matty, of course—but never dreadful, not with you here for him. It's been hard for *you*. I am so sorry. Please forgive me. Let's be a proper family again, OK?' She walked across and put her arms around Lydia. Lydia let her.

'Mum,' she said, her voice quiet in her mother's shoulder. 'I want us to talk to Annie.'

'Annie?'

'Luke and Gideon's mum—kind of—who lives behind us. I want us to tell her everything. We need someone else and I think we need Annie.'

18

'Do it again!' giggled Lydia.

Luke grinned and glanced up the garden to where Jem and Annie and Rebecca Carr, with Matty on her lap, sat in the sun on the veranda, talking and sipping lemonade. He and Gideon shuffled their shoulders together, creating a barrier, and focused their minds on the tea tray between them and Lydia. The dance of the French Fancies continued and a couple of custard creams joined in, pirouetting prettily across the china plate while Gideon hummed a bit of *Swan Lake*.

It was immense fun to share their secret with Lydia. She knew already, of course, because she had seen what Luke had done with his mind in the storm-swept landslip. The other rescuers seemed not to have really taken it in when they were interviewed later. It seemed that none of them had expressed shock or surprise about a semi-conscious boy holding back a chunk of land mass with sheer force of will—not even the white-haired man who had seemed so in command that Lydia had thought maybe he was part of the Control rescue team. He wasn't though. Just a passing good Samaritan. All three of them had said it was just a lucky escape from a landslide according to the Control people who had interviewed her back at home. Either way, it had been a heroic rescue, for which all would be rewarded—very diligently and carefully—by the Cola Project. Lydia, despite the effort of bending her brain around the shock of her mother's return while she was being debriefed, had said nothing about Luke's amazing feat. Instinctively she knew it was best not to.

'Good call,' Gideon agreed, quietly, when she'd told them what had happened. 'It just makes life complicated. *We* know we can trust you not to mention it to anyone. Best that Control stays out of it.'

And of course, once Luke and Gideon knew Lydia knew, it was impossible to avoid showing off just a *little* bit. As they played with cakes and biscuits and then got down to eating them, Lydia told them more about the previous day's events from her own angle.

'That has to go down as one of the freakiest days of my life,' she said. 'First a dead body in the woods, then losing you two and Annie going nuts and telling me the truth about you and then getting Luke back and the storm and the slip and the rescuers and Luke stopping the cliff fall . . . and then all these mad Cola Project people and then going home and finding *Mum* there. *That* was weirdest of all.'

'Must have been pretty freaky for her, too,' observed Gideon, 'walking back into your life on the day you find a body and get caught up in a Cola search-and-rescue.

'Yeah,' said Lydia, glancing back up to the veranda with the tiniest flutter of pride inside her. 'She was incredibly cool in the circumstances. I thought she'd just fall apart but she didn't. She handled the Control people really well. Like a mum should.'

'You think she's going to be OK now, then?' asked Gideon, following her glance. Her mum looked nice. Normal.

'Yeah . . . I think she will,' said Lydia.

The floating cakes hit the plate with a sudden thud as Jem abruptly leapt off the veranda and strode down the garden. He went past them, right to the end, and peered at the fence which backed on to Lydia's. Fish ran down behind him, excited and curious.

At first Gideon thought Jem was checking the security cameras, all now working perfectly again, but he was just tapping on the wood. 'Easy,' called Jem, peering past them at Annie. 'I can probably do it tomorrow before we go, if you've got some tools.'

'Do what?' asked Lydia.

'We were just saying we might as well put a little gate in,' smiled Annie. 'So we don't have to walk all the way round three roads to pop in. We've decided lemonade on the veranda is going to have to be a regular thing.' She raised her tall glass, ice chinking in it, and Rebecca did the same. So did Matty, with his plastic tumbler.

Lydia smiled back at Annie and her mum, understanding. She felt relief trickle through her in slow warm rivulets. It was a feeling she had not had in many months.

'So—about this dream your mum had,' said Gideon. 'What did she say about it again?'

Luke nudged him and signed *Stop it!* but Gideon couldn't resist.

'Oh, that Dad came to her and told her to get it together,' said Lydia.

'Before that,' prompted Gideon.

'Oh—yeah—some blonde girl came first and gave her an earful about getting off her backside and going home. I thought maybe she was just kind of thinking of me . . . but with blonde hair, maybe.'

'Nah,' said Gideon, with a wink at Luke. 'It wasn't you.' He made a mental note to thank Lisa for her help when they got back to Fenton Lodge the next day—and maybe suggest she refine her language a bit. But Lisa never enjoyed hitchhiking into people's minds with the spirit world—it always put her in a bad mood. He was just glad that she'd made the effort.

'FISH!' Lydia was spluttering. The little dog had suddenly arrived at her side and seized a French Fancy in his teeth. He was now running back down the garden with it, casting guilty but delighted glances over his shaggy black shoulder as he went, the pink-iced cube poised daintily in his teeth. It was the funniest thing they'd seen all week and the laughter that rose from the garden was enriched with relief after all the trauma. Even Jem joined in.

Luke woke at 1.15 a.m. on the last day of their holiday with a start. He sat up in bed and re-ran the dream while he could remember it. Catherine again. Burying him alive again. But this time was different. Even *more* different than the last. He had sat up in the shallow grave. He had got to his feet and watched her face go white with shock, the shovel in her hand falling to her feet.

'You're not burying me, Cathy,' he had said—aloud—his voice like Gideon's.

She had gaped at him and tried to pick up her shovel but he had sent it spinning away into the trees.

'You don't have any power over me. Not any more,' he told her and she had edged away from him and then turned into a black raven and flown up into the trees . . . only by the time she reached the branches she was just a lump of black rock and the rock fell back to the ground and split apart,

213

revealing several belemnites. Fossils. Long dead.

Luke got out of bed, smiling, and went to the window. In the holiday let opposite, fresh MI5 minders were manning all the gadgets. He didn't bother to wave, although he felt a pinch of sadness for poor Clara. He glanced across at Gideon, fast asleep, buried in his quilt and said, 'Gid. It's all over. She's gone now. She's just a fossil.'

Gideon gave a little snore.

When Luke woke again in the morning, back in bed, he wasn't sure when the dream had ended. Had he really been able to talk? He tried it . . . but couldn't.

And yet, something had changed. That cold pebble of mistrust inside him. He couldn't feel its weight any more. And maybe his voice would return soon. Maybe.

They said goodbye on the beach below Shanklin Chine. Jem and Annie took Gideon and Luke there on the last day for a big picnic lunch with Lydia, Matty and Rebecca Carr. They had such a good time, running around the sand and splashing through the waves with Fish and Matty, that they barely noticed the *four* MI5 minders backing up Jem.

'Time to go,' said Jem when the picnic had at last been demolished. Annie smiled sadly and started to gather up the leftovers and put them back into the basket.

'We're staying here on the beach a while longer,' said Lydia to Gideon and Luke. 'So . . . this is it. Come on . . . one last paddle.'

They ran back to the water's edge, Luke hobbling slower behind with his left leg in a high-tech plastic brace, and, standing up to her ankles in foamy surf, Lydia dug her hands into her shorts pockets and pulled out two small shiny things. She held them out, one in each palm, to both of them.

'Whoa!' said Gideon, picking up his. It was a beautiful tiny ammonite, fully excavated and almost perfect, apart from some break-through glitter between its ribs.

'Iron pyrites,' said Lydia. 'It gets in and makes it . . . pretty! Luke's is the same . . . but not exactly the same, of course. Like you two, really.'

Luke took his, smiling and peering at it intently through his new glasses. Then he stepped across to

Lydia to give her a hug. She hugged him back and then surprised him by reaching up and kissing him on the cheek.

'You saved my life,' she said. She stepped out of the embrace and then repeated it—and the kiss— for Gideon. 'You saved my life too.'

Luke signed, *Well, you saved mine! We're square!*

'He says you saved his too and you're all square,' grinned Gideon. 'But as you didn't save *mine*, I think I should get another kiss. A proper one!'

Lydia shrieked with pretend horror and slapped his shoulder, but then, very swiftly, she did kiss him on the lips. It was fleeting, but warm and sweet. Gideon went very pink and Luke nearly choked with silent laughter at the sight of him.

'I'm going to miss you weirdos,' said Lydia as they walked back up the beach. 'But I guess I won't need to call now that Mum's back.'

'Yeah, you will,' said Gideon. 'At least twice a week to tell us she's still there.'

'OK,' smiled Lydia. 'I will.'

'And stay away from cliffs!' said Gideon. 'And *you,*' he instructed Fish, who was scrabbling up his knee. 'You *keep* her away from cliffs.'

'Not much chance of that,' said Lydia. 'I'm going

to be a palaeontologist. But maybe I'll steer clear after heavy prolonged rain.'

They left her on the beach, the salty breeze blowing her coppery hair around her face as she waved goodbye, Matty playing with Fish and her mum walking towards her and putting an arm around her.

'Reckon we'll see her again?' sighed Gideon as they got into the new 4 x 4 with Jem and Annie in front. 'I mean . . . isn't that just typical? I get a girlfriend for ten seconds and then it's all over.'

Luke grinned and signed: *We'll see her again. I know it.*

'How do you know it? How do you know they'll ever let us out of Cumbria again?'

Luke signed back, *Look—if you can hold back a speeding bullet . . .*

Gideon allowed himself a flush of pride. 'Yeah . . .' he said. 'Remind me to tell everyone at Fenton Lodge about that, will you?'

Luke laughed and said, 'I won't need to remind you.'

It was nearly a minute before Gideon believed his ears and could tap Annie on the shoulder and tell her.

Ali Sparkes is a journalist and BBC broadcaster who chucked in the safe job to go dangerously freelance and try her hand at writing comedy scripts. Her first venture was as a comedy columnist on *Woman's Hour* and later on *Home Truths*. Not long after, she discovered her real love was writing children's fiction.

Ali grew up adoring adventure stories about kids who mess about in the woods and still likes to mess about in the woods herself whenever possible. She lives with her husband and two sons in Southhampton, England. Check out www.alisparkes.com for the latest news on Ali's forthcoming books.

UNLEASHED

TRICK OR TRUTH
APRIL 2013

Collecting

Darren didn't reply. He hung limply, suspended by his seatbelt, his eyes half closed and his mouth dripping blood. Spook called again, struggling to be free of his own seat belt and the buckled-up seats behind and in front of him. That was when the pain in his wrist went off like a bomb blast and his cries for Darren turned into a shriek of horror.

Pain seemed to brighten all his senses because now he could see properly—which wasn't necessarily a good thing. He could see his left wrist. He could also see the thin rod of metal, burst from the wrecked coach seat, which had skewered right through it. He could see the puffy purple bloom as blood escaped riotously under the pierced skin. On the exit side of the wound it was running down the rod in fast beads like a crimson water feature.

Where were the soldiers? What the hell was going on?

Only minutes ago he and Darren had been slouched in their seats, stretched out on doubles on either side of the aisle in the small coach, talking about Jennifer Troke, the glamourist Darren fancied. The coach was a state-of-the-art armoured vehicle with two armed SAS soldiers inside with them and a third driving—it was more like a prisoner relocation than a day out to a hospital. Spook had seriously expected an RAF helicopter to be tracking them a thousand feet above the winding Cumbrian road—but it seemed the Cola Project had relaxed a bit on that count. Charged with protecting and nurturing more than a hundred Children Of Limitless Ability (and limitlessly useful to their country, Spook never forgot) the Cola project possessed the very best of the most cutting edge surveillance equipment for short- and long-range threat; clearly nobody was expecting any attack today.

So what had *happened*? Spook called out again,

through gritted teeth, trying not to whimper like a girl, in spite of the worst pain he'd ever felt. Nobody responded. Were the soldiers dead? Was *Darren*? What had caused the crash?

RUMBLE . . . His brain now threw up some more images. He'd been glancing out of the window—well, checking his reflection in it, if he was honest—when the first *RUMBLE* caught his attention. Rocks. There were rocks rumbling down the steep fell to the left of the road. An avalanche! High up. So high, he thought, as his brain calculated the odds of danger—swiftly and inaccurately—that they might drive on out of its path in time.

He had heard one of the SAS nannies shout a warning and a responding shout from the driver, even through the bullet-proof glass divide. He hadn't had time to look back at Darren and warn him before the shattering crash. Then the coach was swerving and rolling, brakes screaming, ceiling buckling under the raining rock. And then they were rolling . . . and rolling . . . bodies jarring brutally as gravity and velocity snatched at them and forced them into war with their seat belts. How long this had gone on Spook didn't know. He'd been unconscious when the vehicle came to rest.

'Please . . . someone . . .' whimpered Spook, no longer caring about how he sounded; only that there was someone still to hear him. His wrist felt as if it were being endlessly electrocuted.

Someone came. Nobody he was expecting. But as the pain went swiftly away, Spook really didn't care.

He awoke in a vast bed. A bed so wide and long that he could do a complete 'mattress angel' in it and not feel the edges. The duvet was silky smooth, like satin, and rippled weightlessly as his moving limbs disturbed it. The pillows were satin too, and white. He decided he was probably dreaming. Except for the insistent press on his bladder. He badly needed to urinate. But that could be in the dream too . . .

He gazed around the room, rather hoping the dream would last a while longer, because this room was right up his street. The walls were lined with milk-coloured suede and trimmed with dark wood skirting and cornices. Soft spotlights were set into more suede panels in the low ceiling above him. On either side of the vast bed were dark wood drawer units and each had a broad-brimmed golden parchment lampshade set on a heavy bronze base. The lamps were switched on, adding more golden light to the room.

A shallow glass bowl of red lilies rested on a long low blanket box, of the same dark wood, at the foot of the bed. And off to the right, in a window alcove, was a blue suede two-seater sofa. The three windows above it were round. Folded on the sofa were clothes. Even from this distance Spook could tell that these were also right up his street. Dark turquoise chinos, expensively cut and sleek. A skinny-rib black T-shirt in gleaming fabric, fresh from some opulent store.

This was a *good* dream.

I'll stay here for as long as possible, thought Spook. Because he knew that what was happening in his waking life was not good. Really not good. Involving shock and pain and possibly grief. This dream was a far better place to be, even if he *could* feel some of that pain, seeping in through the fragile membrane of this dream world, from that real world beyond. His wrist twinged. A flash of memory tried for him—*metal—blood*—but he pushed it away and went on looking around the room, trying hard also to ignore the nagging need to pee.

He could smell leather—fine leather, probably Italian. And something cooking somewhere. And the heady scent of the red lilies. Beneath all this, though, was a steady, pervasive fragrance; something he knew well. Fresh, mineral, familiar. It took only the gentle sway of the room that his inner ears were now registering for it to fall into place. The sea. He was at *sea*! In a beautiful, beautiful boat.

Spook sprang up into sitting position and then yelped as a crack of pain registered through his wrist. *Metal! Blood!* The image of his skewered skin shuddered through his mind. DAMN! Now the dream would end and he would wake up back in the coach wreck. DAMN!

He took some steadying breaths, his eyes closed tight, and readied himself for the onslaught of that grim reality from which he'd just been enjoying temporary relief. After a few moments, though, he could still feel the satin across his legs; still smell the lilies, the leather, the cooking, and the sea. He opened his eyes again, his heart thumping. Where the hell *was* he?

As glad as he was not to return to the crash, he was now seriously freaked out. This was no hospital. It was certainly no part of Fenton Lodge. As nice as the dorms were (and he and Darren, privileged as two of the True Eleven, shared one of the best)— this was something *else*.

How had he got here? And when? How long ago? He stared down at his left wrist and saw that it was set in a neat, small cast; sparkling white plaster of Paris holding the no doubt wrecked bones inside immobile. The pain he'd experienced was from the sudden movement of his hand against the cast. It hurt, yes, but barely registered on the scale of pain he'd known in the crash. So . . . He must have been here a while . . . a day? Maybe two? Instinctively he raised his right hand to his chin and upper lip and felt a little soft stubble. Try as he might, growing any kind of stubble took time and what did grow was hardly visible. He barely needed to shave more than once or twice a week—but he *had shaved* on the morning he and Darren had been in the crash. So . . .

Darren. Another thud shook his chest. What had happened to his friend? Darren might not be the best illusionist in the world (how could he be, alongside Spook Williams?) and his bathroom habits left much to be desired . . . but he was the only friend Spook had. That meant something. Was he OK? Or . . . was he . . . *not*?

His legs felt shaky when he tested them, placing his bare feet on the thick cream carpet. He pressed his toes deep into the pile, noting with some relief that he was wearing boxer shorts. None that he recognized, mind you. Dark blue silk. He tried not to think of how they'd got there. If this *wasn't* a dream. And he still hadn't decided about that.

A door was ajar in the left corner of the room, emitting a pale light and a glimmer of pearly tiled wall. He made for it. Inside was a sumptuous bathroom with a circular jacuzzi tub set low into the thickly carpeted floor, a shower in a clear glass tube, echoing the circle of the bath, a circular glass basin beneath a circular mirror and next to this, a circular toilet. Spook lifted its round glass lid and sighed with relief a few seconds later.

Next he splashed water on his face, awkwardly, with one hand, noting a pale bruise on his right cheekbone. Otherwise he looked normal. He found a toothbrush and toothpaste—both clearly unused—and deployed them across his mouth before returning to the cabin.

He walked carefully across to the sofa and stared through the middle porthole. A silver line stretched across the lower half—the handrail of a walkway just outside—and beyond that the deep, fathomless blue of some ocean. Which ocean? Something in its colour and the soft roll of the waves made him doubt it was the North Sea.

Gulping down his fear, which was becoming insistent in the pit of his belly, now that the distracting call of his bladder was settled, Spook picked up the dark turquoise chinos and put them on. They fitted him perfectly; a rare thing for someone so tall and lean. As if they'd been tailored for him. He noticed a belt—a thick weave of golden suede strips and jade wool—and looped it through, doing the bronze clasp up with a satisfying click. The black T-shirt slid on luxuriously. Glancing down he saw no socks, but some black canvas deck shoes with coiled rope soles. He smiled and shook his head without much surprise when he discovered these were a perfect fit too.

Dressed, he felt stronger, although the weakness in his limbs suggested it was a long time since he'd eaten. His stomach gurgled as he took in another lungful of the cooking scent. It smelt like a barbecue . . . roasting steak and onions and peppers. His mouth watered. But all of this was fighting with the deepening sense of panic about where he was. It was time to find out.

He half expected the door to be locked, but although the shining chrome handle was heavy and the door itself weightier still, it opened easily enough. He pulled it wide and stepped up over the dark wood and chrome ridge which rose six inches up from the carpet at the base of the door.

His deck shoe landed on a highly polished wooden walkway, perhaps a metre wide, and a salt-scented breeze ruffled his hair. He grasped the steel rail in front of him, watching the intensely blue water rippling two metres below. He could surely *not* be dreaming this—not with so many senses firing. And now, as if to convince him, his hearing joined in. In the room it had been incredibly quiet, damped by the suede and the satin and the thick carpet. Now he could hear the gentle sigh of the calm sea and the occasional splash against the anchored hull; the breeze passing his face and . . . voices . . . above him. Not far away. His heart lurched. He drew in another steadying breath. It was time to meet some people.

Steps led up to his left. He grabbed the polished chrome rail and followed its tight turn up to the next deck. Arriving on another walkway similar to the one he'd just left, his ears told him the laughter and talk was coming from another level up. He climbed the next curving set of steps, noting the glistening woodwork under his feet; the flawless white of the polished fibreglass beneath the rail; the smell of newness above the perfume of the sea—this boat was fresh. Barely used. And incredibly expensive; his throat beat a pulse of appreciation amid the nerves and the caution and the confusion. He bet it was a Sunseeker; one of the UK's most opulent ocean-going pleasure craft, built just up the coast from his Devon home, over the border in Dorset. It must be, what, forty metres long? Huge. He'd seen one at a boat show a few years back—smaller than this—and had made a mental note that one day he would own one. His father's yacht was pretty impressive, but the Sunseeker . . . it gleamed of wealth and status. And here he was. Aboard the boat of his dreams—but very likely in some kind of nightmare. Wasn't that always the way? He was a Cola after all. Things always turned nightmarish sooner or later.

He reached the sky deck.

There were five people on it. Three men and two women. They didn't notice him for a few seconds as he stood, gripping the top of the stairwell railing. One man, in white chef's fatigues, was attending to the barbecue, flipping thick steaks and adjusting a line of pepper and mushroom kebabs. Next to him a plump, middle-aged woman in a white blouse and black skirt was opening a bottle of what looked like champagne. They both looked Mediterranean, with dark hair and olive skin. A short distance away from the staff, a tall lean man with blond hair and a deep tan lay stretched out on a white leather sun lounger, wearing only shorts. He was engrossed in lively conversation with another older man who had dark grey hair and was perched on the edge of a neighbouring lounger, wearing what appeared to be a captain's uniform, minus the hat. Between these two, apparently oblivious to the conversation, reclined a girl in a lime-green bikini. Her long dark hair rippled past her shoulders and was occasionally played with by the gentle sea breeze. She had mirror sunglasses on, disguising her eyes, but her skin was golden and flawless and her full mouth was painted with red lipstick.

And she must have had her eyes open behind the shades, because she was the first one to sit up, prodding the lean, blond-haired man as she did so, and nodding towards the new arrival. The man sat up too, twisting towards him, and a smile—which seemed oddly familiar—broke out across his face.

'Hello, Spook,' he said. 'I'm so pleased you've joined us.'